ULRICH
Elemental's CT MC
(book 1)

ALEXI FERREIRA

ULRICH
Elementals CT MC (Book 1)

Copyright © 2020 Alexi Ferreira
All rights reserved.

No part of this publication may be reproduced, distributed, or transmitted in any form or by any means, including photocopying, recording, or by other electronic or mechanical methods, without the prior written permission of the author, except in the case of brief quotations embodied in used critical reviews and certain other non-commercial uses as permitted by copyright law. For permission requests, write to the author, mentioning in the subject line:

"Reproduction Request" at the address below:

alexiferreira.writer@gmail.com

This book is a work of fiction and any resemblance to any person or persons, living or dead, any event, occurrence, or incident is purely coincidental. The characters and story lines are created and thought up from the author's imagination or are used fictitiously.

https://alexiferreirawrite.wixsite.com/mysite

Amazon.com/author/alexiferreira

Facebook.com/alexiferreira.writer

Someday, someone will walk into your life and make you realize why it never worked with anyone else.

Contents

ULRICH 1 9
ANASTASIA 2 20
ULRICH 3 30
ANASTASIA 4 40
ULRICH 5 52
ANASTASIA 6 63
ULRICH 7 75
ANASTASIA 8 86
ULRICH 9 98
ANASTASIA 10 108
ULRICH 11 121
ANASTASIA 12 132
ULRICH 13 143
ANASTASIA 14 153
ULRICH 15 163
ANASTASIA 16 176
ULRICH 17 187
ANASTASIA 18 199
ULRICH 19 213
A MESSAGE FROM ALEXI FERREIRA 222
DANE 1 223

ALEXI FERREIRA

ACKNOWLEDGMENTS

Thank you to my children that believe in me and have stood by me every step of the way, and to my readers for all their support without all of you this dream wouldn't be possible.

And a big thank you to all the A's Guardians, I am blessed to have such unbelievable support from such amazing women, and a very special thank you to Mikki and Sydnee for all your hard work and dedication you keep me grounded.

ULRICH 1

"Ulrich, fuck get your ass out of bed." Cracking one eye open I see Garth standing in the open doorway, "Tor is waiting downstairs, and he's in a foul mood today." Shit, I forgot we were riding out. Turning, I am attacked with a mop of brown hair. Argh, I forgot they were here. Sitting up, I first look to one side seeing Tracy and then to the other to see Monica both fast asleep.

"One of these days you going to wear that pecker of yours to the bone." At Garth's sarcastic comment I grin as I climb over Tracy to pick up my Jeans on the ground, kicking a pair of panties out of the way with my foot.

"That might have just happened last night, I swear I heard the word bone quite a lot."

"Fucker, just get a move on or Tor is going to have both our heads." The last thing I feel like now is to deal with Tor's thunder as we call it. He is one mean son of a bitch when things don't go his way. "I swear one of these days he's going to place you on guard duty, then your bone will rot," Garth mutters as he turns to walk out of the room. I finish lacing up my boots and then pulling a t-shirt out of my drawer I follow Garth, picking my Kutte off the chair that is next to the door, I slip the t-shirt on as we make our way downstairs.

We have been trying to combat the skin trade here in Cape Town for a couple of years, but every time we bring down a gang another fucking gang pops up. We know that there are still some of the Keres that we haven't been able to find and bring in, we are sure they are the ones that are behind this whole organization, but every time we think we have found their leader he disappears.

As elemental's we each have the power of a specific element, before we found a way of calming our fury so as not to turn into Keres. Keres were the elemental's that turned into darkness, evil, they still had powers but muted. Since finding the cure that we have been able to bring some of the Keres back, but some are crafty and manage to get away from us as they know what we can and cannot do.

"Did you not hear me when I said eight," Tor says in a quiet voice as we walk into the bar area, there are still people lying around from last night's party, at his raised voice some mumble and open their eyes. His arms are tense as he crosses them, his eyes flashing in anger. Tor is a scary son of a bitch when he's angry, but he will also lay down his life for anyone of us, which we in turn would do for each other and him too.

Throughout my very long three hundred and forty-six years of life, the best years have been the ones since I have been with the Elemental's MC and that is all thanks to Tor, he thought I deserved a chance and gave it to me. He didn't make it easy; I had to work for my spot at his side, but I have never regretted it.

"Sorry man, I only got to sleep a couple of hours ago," I mutter remembering Tracy and Monica that are still upstairs in my bed.

"Well, seeing as you can't be responsible after going to a party, you are banned from the next one," I grunt, but don't complain as it could have been much worse. I will just make sure to keep out of his radar for the rest of the day and I should be fine. At least he didn't ban me from women for a month like he did once before. "Let's fucking leave, we have wasted enough time here already," he mutters as he turns and stalks out of the club.

"You got it easy Bro," Colborn says as he walks past me,

"I would have torched your ass," he quips

"You would have tried," I reply with a grin as I follow them outside. Walking towards my bike, I smile; Garth must have picked up the panties when I kicked them away from my Jeans because there they are hanging from my handlebars like a flag. "Very funny," I say as I look at him to see a wide grin on his face before he slides the helmet on.

Tucking the panties into my jeans pocket I Pull my kutte on over my t-shirt, leaning forward I pick up my helmet from my seat. Riding a bike is part of who I am, there is nothing like feeling the wind on your face or the thrill that I get when I speed down a road. As I start my bike I groan, shit I forgot my weapons in the room because of being late. Hopefully, I'm not going to need them because Tor will have my head for sure if that happens.

Being an Elemental I am privileged to be the element of fire, if need be I will fight using my element but when we are out in the open we try not to, as humans don't know about us and we want to maintain it like that. Dag, Eirik and Tal must have stayed behind, making sure that everyone that came to the party leaves as I don't see them riding ahead. Opening the throttle to my bike, I let everything melt away as I ride around the twisty bends on the roads, sea breeze blowing around me as I follow the others to our destination.

We received information that one of the gangs might

have picked up two women yesterday and they will be transporting them soon, therefore we need to act quickly before they ship them. We know that they are shipping the women in containers out of the country, but we haven't been able to find the source, we have stopped quite a lot of women from being trafficked but as soon as they are on those ships or ship they are gone.

We have two gangs that we have persuaded in working with us, but we had to agree on supplying them with weapons. We know that we can't trust them fully, but they are aware that if we find out that they are still kidnapping women and trafficking them, then we won't be merciful. Where we are going today was a tip from one of those gangs, We have agreed to split up when we get there just in case this is an ambush, for their own health I sure hope it isn't because we will go after each one in that gang and make sure they never cross us again.

When we are a couple of blocks away Tor pulls over indicating with his hand for the others to continue. Garth, Colborn, Haldor and I continue while the others pull up and park their bikes. They will be following us on foot. When we are but a block away, we park our bikes when we see the leader of the gang that we are here to meet leaning against his yellow pimped-up car.

He raises his hand in greeting as he approaches, "they are still in there, I have two of my boys keeping an eye on them," he says, "It looks like there might be about five men inside or close by."

"Thanks, you can pull your men back and leave, we will take it from here," Haldor says as he gets off his bike.

"You will let Tor know that I was here?" Basil asks, last time Tor went to visit Basil he filled him with enough fear to make him think twice about crossing us.

"Yeah, he will know" Colborn says as the four of us start making our way on foot down the road. We are nearly at the house when we see the two men Basil mentioned making their way to where Basil was. It is clear that they don't like us but that is fine as we are not here to make friends, the only thing we want is to stop the trafficking as most of the women that are being kidnapped are women that have specific gifts, women that are usually a match with one of the elemental's.

As Elemental's we only have one true mate, the one that calms the fury in our souls that enhances our element and that brings us happiness and peace. Most of us go through centuries without meeting our mate, that is why so many turned Keres and joined the Keres MC before Draco and his men started by bringing down their MC and helping the Keres back into their Elemental state and find their mates.

To be honest, I'm not in a rush to find my mate, I'm enjoying life way too much, I know what some brothers have said about how different it is once we find that one woman and how she changes our life, but that's what I don't want, I don't want a woman to come into my life and start telling me what to do and not to do. It was different before, when our fury took the best of us and we turned, but ever since finding a cure I don't see a need to find that one woman.

I smile to myself when I think of the two women back at the club in my bed, yip, not in a hurry to be shackled. When we are but a couple of houses away Garth and I walk through one of the houses driveways to the back garden and then over the wall into the other house. We walk through that garden until we reach the wall, taking a breath I jump, holding the top with my hands I swing over it and land on the other side on top of a fucking sprinkler that immediately starts to shoot out water.

"Fuck," I mutter, hurrying away from the spray. I see Garth grinning as he shakes his head in amusement. We make our way towards the housekeeping to the shadows, stopping when we see a shadow by one of the windows. Garth leans down placing his hands flat on the grass, his head slightly tilted as he feels the vibration on the ground, Garth bends the element earth which in this case is handy as he can sense how many people might be inside the house.

He lifts his hand, showing me five. If what Basil said is to be believed then two of those vibrations are the women and the other three must be the men holding them. I nod and make my way towards the side of one of the windows. I can hear someone talking, must be on the phone as there is no reply. There is a TV that is on, a kettle that I can hear which tells me that at least one of them is in the kitchen. I look over at Garth standing at the other window and nod; he walks towards the back sliding door, tugging he opens it back and quickly enters I follow to find Garth already by the guy that was on his phone, his arm around his neck from behind as he subdues him.

I make my way towards the kitchen; I don't know what it is with this house, but my senses are all over the fucking place. Just before I reach the kitchen a big son of a bitch comes around the corner. When he sees me, he throws the mug that he is holding at me and then charges. I feel the hot liquid touching my skin, but I don't flinch as I prepare for his attack. I see Colborn and Haldor have come in through the front door, one is hurrying downstairs while the other disappears into a room further down the corridor.

I squat down just as the guy throws a punch, my fist flying up and hitting him in the gut, which has him trying to catch his breath. Standing up straight I throw another punch, this one hitting him on the cheek which has his head snapping to the left as he stumbles back and finally falls. I walk up to him, tapping him with the toe of my boot, but he doesn't move. Grunting I make my way towards where I see Colborn now going downstairs, these humans are no fun you punch them once and they are out like a light. I can hear fighting from outside which tells me that Tor and the others must have found the men outside and are subduing them.

"It's okay sweetheart we are here to help you." I hear Haldor saying as I come around the curve in the stairs to encounter a basement littered with soiled matts on the floor, at least six of them, which tells me that at some time or another there have been other women here. I don't know what it is about this house, but it has my skin crawling as if all the blood is rushing just under it. "Colborn see to the other one," Haldor says just as I reach the bottom. The lighting in here is dim, and the smell is putrid, but we will soon have these poor women out of here and into fresh air.

"Get away from me," I hear a hoarse voice say, which has me stopping dead. What the fuck is that, it feels like I just got punched in the gut, my breath is choppy, my heart has started to race and my vision has sharpened as if I'm about to go into battle. Is this some kind of gift that this woman has, maybe her gift is to get men into battle readiness, but when I look at Colborn and Haldor they seem unaffected.

"We are going to get you out of here, we are the good guys," Haldor consoles, I try to see the woman from where I'm standing but Haldor is in the way. Colborn has picked up the other woman that is unconscious and is carrying her upstairs. I approach Haldor and the woman. The closer I get the more my senses seem to calm. I wonder what her gift is because it's playing haywire with me, I thought Draco had said that these women's gifts didn't work on us, well I don't think he encountered this one before.

And then Haldor moves slightly and everything around me seems to still, "Fuck no," I mutter which has Haldor glance behind him a frown on his face as he looks at me. I don't think she hears me but at Haldor's move she looks up at me and then I see her eyes widen slightly. She has the lightest sky-blue eyes that I have ever seen, her pale complexion contrasting to her pitch-black hair. I can see freckles speckled across the bridge of her nose, her features are delicate, feminine and so beautiful. The bruise on her forehead evident with her light complexion, there are also bruises on her arms and throat as if someone tried to strangle her. Oh, fuck no. Maybe if I turn around and leave, everything will go back to normal.

"I will go with him," she says, lifting her hand and pointing at me. No, no, no, I close my eyes trying to dispel this feeling of protection, of possessiveness that is overtaking my senses, my system. This can't be happening. Just an hour ago I was thinking of how perfect my life was and now fate threw me with this curve ball. I feel every single fibre in my body coming to life, racing through my body.

"No problem, sweetheart, Ulrich will help you upstairs," Haldor says as he turns and heads towards me, a frown on his face as he looks at me. His longish blond hair falling forward over his eye, which has him lifting his hand to stroke his fingers through it, pulling it back. "What's up?" he asks with a raised brow when he's standing before me.

"I'm fucked."

ANASTASIA 2

I don't know what they have been giving me, but my head is woozy, and everything is still moving around. I don't know how long it has been now since they kidnapped me from outside my home, but ever since then that they have moved me three times. I don't know if it's day or night any longer as there are no windows down here, I don't even know where I am.

At first, I still fought but then they started sedating me. Now I'm just too drained to do anything at all. I move my head on the matt I'm laying on to look across at the other matt where Dora is laying. I don't even know if she's still alive, I met her when they moved me into the second location, she was very quiet, withdrawn and hardly spoke but for a while now that she has not said a word. I know that she hasn't been eating either because I heard one of the men muttering to himself when he came to get our plates.

Not that I blame her. All we have been getting to eat since being taken is two slices of bread with butter and water. I have pushed myself to eat everything and drink as much water as I can; I want to be ready when the gap comes for me to find a way out of this situation. Then I shake my head at myself as I think of what I am considering, how far would I make it, unless they stop injecting me with whatever they have been giving me I won't be able to make it anywhere. I move first one leg side to side and then the other.

How did I get into this situation? Why would they want to take me? I ask for the millionth time. At the beginning I asked the men that held me, but I never got a reply, instead I got smacked around a few times. I tried to run the first day I was caught, that didn't go too well as I was knocked unconscious. I just want to know what they are planning on doing with us. Why are they keeping us in this limbo for so long? If they have taken us for the sex trade shouldn't they be taking better care of us?

Dora won't be able to do much, that is, even if she is still alive. Even my weird gift that I have had ever since I was a teenager has deserted me. I lift my hand trying to manifest the coldness, the ice that I could so easily manifest at a simple whim. Now nothing happens. I place both hands flat besides me and push myself up until I am sitting up; I lean against the wall behind me, until my back is flush against the wall. The coolness of the wall penetrating my very dirty clothes, cooling me down.

I have been wearing the same yellow dress ever since they took me, at one time this was my favourite dress, now I would give anything to burn it and wear anything else. It is browner than yellow now, there is a tear on the skirt, and it smells.

I wonder what people must be thinking about my disappearance, Mr. Smith must be climbing the walls. He won't know where anything is in the office as I am the one that does everything for him, as his personal assistant he makes sure to use me to my full potential, but I don't mind as I know I am good at what I do and I am pleased that he trusts me enough to leave most of the things in my hands.

At first I didn't think that I would work for him for very long as he came across as a real perv, but I soon put him in his place and he turned out to be a sweet man. He pays me well but after working for him for five years he knows that he can leave the office and things won't fall apart. I'm a fixer, my personality excels at fixing problems, the fact that I can't find a way out of this situation has my head in a knot.

My parents would have realized that I am missing and

would have gone to the police by now. Are they looking for me? What will the worry of not knowing what happened to me do to my dad? He has a weak heart and I just pray that this doesn't push him over the edge into getting another heart attack.

Maybe if I had a man in my life, this wouldn't have happened, maybe he would have gone to pick me up at work. Most women at twenty-six already have a man in their lives but not me. Apparently, I'm too strong willed for most men. I always thought that one day I would meet the perfect man for me, that he would understand that I am my own person, that he wouldn't try to control me but be my partner. I don't believe in being owned; I believe in equal rights.

I'm like any other woman, I like to be pampered by a man; I like the attention and the sweet words but I want to be able to also contribute. I want to be able to also treat him and pamper him if I feel like it; I want him not to be bothered with the fact that I earn more than him if that is the case but everyone I have met till now has been the absolute opposite of what I am looking for.

Now I might never meet anyone that will love me, someone that I can love in return. I think every woman thinks of that epic love story that we meet that one person that loves us unconditionally with all our faults and that they understand us and don't judge us when we in one of our moods because of our periods or because we wake up in a bad mood, does that even exist or is it all a fantasy that we all tell ourselves just to feel better and keep the dream going?

I hear a noise, my eyes open but there is no one, the overhead light is dim which helps to hide some filth in this area. I wonder how many women have been in this basement, how many women have been taken from their loved ones, from their families and brought into a life of sadness, of pain and maybe that is even dead by now.

I feel tears behind my eyes threatening to fall but I hold them at bay, I will not give up hope, I will not give in. I lift my arm and wince at the pain in my joints, my hand moves to my hair to pull it away from my face and I wince again at the knots that I feel in it. My hair is always a problem to untangle because of how curly it is but now with all this time going by and with it not being washed or combed I will never be able to take the knots out.

Dropping my hand to my lap once again I look at it, since I was a teenager that I have been able to lower my body temperature to the point where I can freeze liquid or little ice particles appear on my fingers. At first, I was scared when I realized that I was different, that others can't do what I do. My parents were concerned and took me for tests, but I was told that nothing was wrong with me and I was a rarity where I could drop my body temperature. They wanted to do more tests on me to try and find out how I can do this, but my parents stopped it.

They warned me not to tell anyone because others might not understand, and they were right, I told a boyfriend of mine once and at first he seemed to accept it but with time he started to say that my heart was made of ice, that I was incapable of loving anyone and all because I would not conform to his way of wanting me to be. He wanted me to jump when he said jump and live my life according to what he thought was right and I couldn't do that as I have always had a mind of my own even when I was young.

Needless to say, I never told another soul again, and now it seems like I will never need to say anything again as it looks like I can't cool myself down any longer. The cold of the wall seeping into my back gives me some comfort, but I still feel like my insides are burning.

"Dora," I call, my voice is slightly breathless but audible, "Dora, wake up," she doesn't move but I think I see her stomach moving slightly which tells me that she must still be alive. I hear another noise, this one on the stairs that leads down here, my body tensing as I think of the assholes that I have seen, it's most probably bread and water time.

When a man comes into sight I frown, this one is new, I haven't seen him before. He doesn't have that evil feeling like the others do. His hair is a longish blond, looking windblown, his blue eyes seem to take everything in as he looks around. Even though he doesn't have the evil feeling to him he seems much more dangerous than any of the other men I have seen here before.

"Is it only the two of you in here?" I frown at his question. What is he playing at, does he see anyone else here? When I don't answer he frowns as he approaches, looking at Dora as he passes, "Do you understand me?" he asks as he squats down before me.

"I'm not stupid," I mutter which has him smiling, this man is dangerous to every woman out there his smile is dazzling and makes me want to confide in him, which will just make me do the opposite.

"That's good to know," he says in amusement, "I am here to help you."

"Of course, you are," I say sarcastically, which has his smile disappearing and a frown take its place. I hear more footsteps coming down the stairs and even though I try to see behind him, his chest is so wide that I can't see who has just come down.

"It's okay sweetheart we are here to help you," he says, and then he glances back over his shoulder and points to Dora, "Colborn see to the other one." When he looks back at me he stretches out his hand towards mine which has me flinching back, I don't care what he says, I don't trust him, there have been way too many of these assholes trying to be friends ever since they took me, for me to believe in him.

"Get away from me," I say and see him tense.

"We are going to get you out of here, we are the good guys," he says in a quiet voice, but I shake my head as I see another man picking up Dora. Is he saying the truth, are they really here to help us?

And then he moves slightly and everything around me seems to still as I see a man standing a few feet behind him. He has the kindest eyes I have ever seen and even though he is as handsome as they come with straight brown hair that touches his shoulders. A stubble that must be so erotic when he kisses, and the naughtiest look to him that spells trouble, I am somehow drawn to him. He seems hesitant, as if he would rather just turn and leave right now.

"I will go with him," I say, lifting my hand and pointing to the man standing behind him. To my surprise, I see the man take a step back as if he would rather do anything else instead of taking me out of here.

"No problem, sweetheart, Ulrich will help you upstairs," the man before me says, as he stands up straight and then turns heading towards the man. What kind of name is Ulrich? I see him say something and the man reply but I can't hear their interaction and then the man that was before me looks back at me with a surprised look on his face.

What the hell is going on? The man seems to straighten his shoulders and then he is stepping towards me, a scowl now on his face as if he's not happy about doing this, well that's just too bad isn't it? When he is before me, he places an arm under my legs and then another behind me and picks me up. The sudden movement has my muscles complaining, which has me groaning in pain. He freezes with me halfway up, "Fuck," he mutters, "I'm sorry," the uncertainty in his face has me feeling sorry for him, the poor man seems to be appalled at my pain.

"It's okay Ulrich," I say and feel his arms tighten slightly as he pulls me the rest of the way up and against his chest. I don't know if what the other guy said is true and they are here to help me but all I know is that in this man's arms I am feeling safe, safe for the first time in a long time.

"What's your name?" his voice is low and deep, like hot chocolate in a cold evening running over my body, giving me comfort in a strange kind of way. I lean my head against his chest hearing his heart, closing my eyes as everything starts to spin around me. He definitely lifted me up way too quickly.

"Anastasia," and then I feel myself start to shake, what the hell is happening to me?

"Fuck," I hear Ulrich saying and then we seem to be rushing upstairs, my head seeming to feel lighter and lighter with each minute that passes. "Get out of the fucking way, where's Tor?" I hear him say as I seem to be drifting in and out of consciousness, my teeth chattering.

"Blood," I seem to hear someone say and then there is a burst of intense sweetness in my mouth just as I start feeling myself being dragged down to darkness. I tighten my hand around Ulrich's t-shirt, he needs to stay with me, I know I will be fine if he stays with me.

ULRICH 3

"Tor," I bellow as I rush out of the house, relieved when I see him walking up the path to the front door. Anastasia in my arms convulsing, I can feel her body in my arms shaking, getting worse by the minute.

"What the fuck?" Tor mutters as he sees us.

"She's mine, she's fucking mine." I know I must seem like a complete idiot but she's in my arms convulsing what the hell must I do? Aren't mates supposed to know what to do to help their mates? Maybe I'm wrong, maybe she's not mine. I look down at her and see her eyes closed, her complexion milky white, and I'm frozen like an idiot.

"Ulrich look at me," Tor snaps, my eyes rise to meet his, he has stopped a couple of feet away from us his eyes intense as he looks at me. "Now take a breath and calm down, all your woman needs is your blood." Blood, of course how the hell did I forget that? Stepping back, I take a seat on the step to the house before raising my wrist to my mouth and tearing at it with my teeth.

"Anastasia, open up," I mutter as I place my wrist near her lips, "It's all going to be okay now." A couple of drops coat her lips and enter her mouth. "Swallow," I mutter. It takes a little while, but she finally starts to calm. I take in a deep breath feeling the air rushing into my lungs, looking up I see Tor is still standing where he was, his arms crossed as he waits.

We should have picked the women up and been out of here by now, but he waited until I calmed Anastasia. I nod thanking him, I can still feel my hand shaking from the adrenalin rushing through my body. I haven't felt that type of adrenalin in a very long time. A grin splits across his face, and then he throws back his head and roars with laughter. Dane comes to stand behind him, a surprised look on his face.

"I don't see where the joke is," I mutter.

"The joke is that you can go to the next party, your life has just become a lot more interesting and I don't want to miss any of it," Tor says with a grin as he inclines his head towards Anastasia in my arms.

"She will be good," I mutter only to hear Haldor snort as he walks past me, looking up I glare at him as he shoulder bumps Tor with a grin.

"The way she was back chatting me in there, he has just met his match." I glare at Haldor. She was simply scared, and what the hell am I thinking I'm not going to keep her. I look down at her and feel a sense of familiarity, a feeling of belonging that I haven't felt before. Shit, I need to get away from her and quickly.

"Ulrich get her in that van, I think it's the one they used. We will dispose of it later." I look over at the van and then at Haldor, I'm about to tell Haldor to take her but a feeling of anger overwhelms me at the thought of him touching her. Damn, I stand moving towards the van where I see that Colborn has already placed the other woman. Placing her on her back on the floor of the van I start to straighten only to find her fingers holding onto my t-shirt, she must be scared, out of her mind, we should kill every single one of those assholes inside but I know that Tor will want to question them first.

"You want to drive brother?" Colborn asks as he walks past, I gently undo her fingers stroking them before placing her hand next to her.

"No, you drive. I will stay here to help with the interrogations." Colborn stops and turns to look at me, a frown on his face.

"I thought she was your mate," he says

"She is, but maybe if I don't take her blood the bond will just simmer until we are ready to commit to each other." At my statement, Colborn's eyebrows rise in surprise and then he shakes his head.

"You know that's not going to happen don't you, the mating has already started, and the feelings of urgency will simply grow the longer you leave it." At his statement I grunt, not everyone is the same, maybe ours will simmer for a while. I shrug as I turn to walk back inside, I see Colborn shake his head as he walks towards the driver's seat.

Tor raises a brow when he sees me walking in, he is leaning against one of the walls seeing Dane questioning the one guy. "Like that is it?" he asks as I come to stand next to him

"I'm just not ready," I mutter.

"Well, I hate to tell you this, but you better hurry up and get ready because from what I hear it doesn't give you much of a choice." I know what he says is true but I'm not ready to hang up my single status yet, so instead of answering I simply shrug. "You just prolonging the inevitable, and from what I've heard it's not too bad being mated." At his statement, I look at him with an unbelievable expression.

"Really, you are telling me that being mated is fine. You Tor that swears by being single." He grins and then winks.

"I'm telling you what I've heard, I'm not telling you how I feel about it, but to be honest I think she will be good for you."

"You are joking?" I state looking at him suspiciously

"No, you are spiralling out-of-control Ulrich. You think I don't know about the rotation of woman that goes through your room, or the fights you are getting into. You are losing your cool more than normal, it's not just because of the life we lead, it's because something is missing that you can't fill the void of and you are filling it with the wrong things." He lifts his arm placing his hand on my shoulder as he looks directly at me, "I believe that she has come at the right time, because I was thinking of sending your ass to Draco."

"I'm fine," I mutter but I know that what he is saying is true, but I'm not one to be controlled or leashed into submission like a woman might want to do. An image of Anastasia fills my mind which has me instantly hard, her delicate features laying against my chest so defenceless. The knowledge that she has been through a hard time at the hands of these bastards has my fury rising.

"Let me go at them," I mutter, looking at the other men in one of the corners of the room.

"No," I glance at Tor in surprise

"Why not?"

"Because I can feel your anger and I would rather have them tell us what they know then you kill them outright," I grunt and move towards where Dane is questioning the asshole that thinks it's okay to take women from their lives into this.

"How many places like this are there?" Dane asks only to have the guy spit, Dane smiles and then he is pulling back his arm and punches him in the gut that has the guy snapping forward as he fights for breath. "Let's try again, how many more places like this are there?"

"I don't know, fuck," he mutters as he still gasps for air, "we drive to an area, collect the van with the girls and come here." That is the same story that most of them are telling us. There must be someone that knows more than he is saying.

I look towards the group of guys, "where are their phones?" I ask, remembering that one was on the phone when we came in.

"Here," Einar says holding up his hands with about seven phones in them.

"Have you checked them?" I ask.

"They all locked, we can get Celmund to check." Everything tech related we send to Celmund, he is part of the brothers in Draco's group and one hell of hacker but it might be too late as the asshole that was on the phone might have been making plans as we entered.

35

Looking at the group again I see the guy, he is leaning against the wall his mouth bleeding and a bruise on his forehead but other than that he looks good.

"Give me those," taking them I walk up to the asshole, "which one is yours?" He just glares at me so I pick up the first one pressing the side button. I see it's locked so I point it at his face, nothing happens, pulling his hand I place his index finger at the back but the phone doesn't unblock. I try another and another until I get to the fourth one. As soon as I point it at his face, the phone comes on.

"There we go, thank you," I mutter sarcastically as I stand on his hand as I get up. I go through his calls seeing the number he was on as we came in, then I go to his messages. "Well, look what we have here," I mutter walking towards Tor with the phone.

I hold up the phone to Tor for him to see the message that is organizing a drop off of the woman at the pier tonight. "Finally," Tor mutters as he nods. We have been trying to find which ship company they are using or if private owners, now we might just find who they are. He pulls out his phone and dials, "Tal, when Colborn gets there he must drop the women, turn around and bring that van back." He listens to something and then, "yeah, we might have a lead, chat later," and then he's pocketing his phone.

"Hasn't Colborn arrived yet?" he should have been at

the club by now. Was there a problem? I can feel a knot tightening in my stomach at the thought that something might have happened.

"He has just arrived," Tor says with a knowing look which has me wanting to kick myself, damn, she's already getting under my skin and I haven't even completed our bond yet. Ever since touching her my mind has been on her but that's normal isn't it? I'm curious to know what kind of mate I got.

"Dane, you and Einar stay here and keep on working these fuckers, the rest of us have somewhere to be." Tor turns to me and inclines his head to the outside door, "go tell Asger to get the others ready and what's going on."

I make my way outside to see Asger on the other side of the road near a tree, if anyone comes from one side of the road or the other he will see and has a chance to hide in case they are watching this place. "What's up?" Asger asks when I approach.

"We have got a lead, Colborn is bringing the Van back and then we are riding to the pier. Looks like they were dropping the women off there today." Asger punches my arm playfully.

"Aren't you lucky, if we had come tomorrow you would never have found your mate." At his words I frown, I might not have wanted to find my mate at the moment but I would never have wanted her to be trafficked somewhere, the thought of what could have happened to her has my vision sharpening in anger. "Hey, no harm done brother relax, you have her now."

"This wasn't supposed to happen yet," I mutter and see Asger frown.

"You are three hundred and something years old, don't you think you have played the field enough?" Asger asks.

"Does anyone ever play enough?" I state with a wink, trying to shed light on the matter.

"Ulrich you have always run away from responsibility, this is a big thing for you. You are now going to have a woman that you are responsible for, you are going to have to think of someone else besides the club and us, someone that is your responsibility as this is a dangerous life we lead. That brother," he places a hand on my shoulder, "is what you are fighting against and not your mate." And with those words he drops his hand and starts walking away to go and tell the others what is happening.

"You must stop being such a philosopher," I mutter after him, Asger has always been the voice of reason, he will analyse everything until exhaustion or until it finally makes sense to him. I hear him chuckle as he walks away, I raise my hand showing him the finger even though he has his back to me and doesn't see it, it makes me feel better.

Darn, what he says makes sense. I really hate change, and I hate responsibility. Grunting I lean against the tree pulling out my smokes. I light one while I wait for the others. I hope this doesn't take long, I want to find the assholes that are trafficking the women and bring down who's responsible for shipping them, but everything in me is telling me to go back to the club and make sure that Anastasia is fine.

Anastasia, I say the name again in my head, liking the way it makes me feel. She has a beautiful name; I think it suits her. She seems so defenceless, so small, her body fits against mine perfectly, I try to dispel the thought of her body or her face as I have had a hard-on ever since I touched the woman. The Elemental's that have bonded I have always heard them say that there is no sex that can compare to having sex with their mates.

That is something that I am curious about, but if the way my body has reacted to her is any indication then I think that everything that I have heard might be true. She looked so angelic even with the bruises and the dirt, how can anyone hurt someone that angelic?

ANASTASIA 4

I open my eyes to find myself on a proper bed, turning my head I see a window. Where am I? and then I remember the men coming down the stairs. Wait, where is he? I raise my head and groan as it swirls, well looks like I'm still not back to myself but if I am truly free from those men, then I should be back to health soon. Maybe they will let me call my parents and I will need to let Mr. Smith know what happened.

"I see you are awake." I jump at the voice, looking towards the bottom of the bed I see a man walking into the room. What the hell, am I hallucinating? Yesterday the man that was talking to me was hot, then Ulrich was drop dead scalding hot, and now this guy is just as hot.

ULRICH

I'm sure I must be dreaming.

"Are you real?" At my question he grins, okay now I'm sure I'm dreaming because a smile like that can't belong to a real guy.

"I think so." If old whiskey had a voice, I'm sure it would sound like this guy, raspy and hot.

"You're hot," I say and see both his eyebrows raise as his grin widens.

"Well thank you, just do me a favour and don't tell Ulrich that okay?" At his statement I frown

"Is he real?" I ask

"Well, honey sometimes I wonder, but it seems like he is." I frown at his cryptic answer. What does he mean with that? "I hear your name is Anastasia, how are you feeling?"

"Umm, okay," I mutter, "just confused and I think dizzy, where am I?" And my whole body still hurts but I won't tell him that.

"You're in our club, the doctor has been to see you and Ulrich is downstairs arguing with him, but he should be back upstairs soon." At Ulrich's name, my stomach seems to somersault.

"What do you mean?" Either my brain is only working at half capacity or this man is cryptic as hell.

"You weren't waking up which was freaking Ulrich out, we rescued you yesterday in the morning, it is now two in the afternoon." Wow, did I really sleep for that long?

"What's your name?" I ask.

"What an asshole, we should really get another fucking doctor," Ulrich is saying angrily as he walks into the room. The minute I see him, it feels like the bottom of my stomach has dropped; he is even more handsome than I remembered. His longish brown hair just touching his shoulders seems dishevelled, like his fingers have been through it a few times. His beautiful green eyes snapping in anger as he looks at the man that I was talking to. His arms are muscular and tattooed, he looks like the perfect picture of naughty. There is no doubt in my muddled brain that this man is trouble in every sense of the word.

"Look who has woken up while you were arguing with the doctor." At the man's words Ulrich's gaze snaps around to me and I see relief in his features.

"Hi," I say and see his lips twitch.

"Did you have a nice nap?" he asks with a raised brow as he walks towards me, his t-shirt stretched across his muscular chest. Darn, but this man makes me dribble even when I'm feeling like a sick dog.

"Yes, thank you," I murmur feeling suddenly self-conscious, I look towards where the other guy was only to find him gone. "What was the name of the guy that was here?" I see him suddenly frown.

"Haldor, why?"

"What kind of name is Haldor, does that stand for something?" he shakes his head his frown still in place.

"His name is an old Norse name; it is just Haldor. You will find that all of us here have old Norse names."

"Oh, did you all change your original names to fit in with the club or something?" I have heard of bikers with strange nicknames, but I have never encountered ones that change their names to Norse ones. He takes a seat on the bed, his knee but a hand's length away, completely distracting me from what I was talking about.

"No, we were all born with them." My eyes rise to his, the green flecks in his eyes capturing my attention. It should be illegal for someone to be this handsome. "You haven't said why you want to know his name?" I frown and then shrug.

"No reason, he was just so nice," I mutter suddenly yawning, I can see his eyes taking everything in. "What did the doctor say?"

"That the bruising will go away and that whatever they were pumping into your system will wear off soon and then you will start to feel better," he says, "How are you feeling, are you in any pain?"

"No, I'm actually feeling better than what I have felt for days." He nods, "Ulrich," I stretch out my hand placing mine on top of his, jumping in surprise when we both get shocked with static. I can feel every fibre in my body responding to the touch, I know that my system is run down and at the moment I am more than likely feeling everything more intensely than I usually would but this man has me reacting in a way that I have never felt before. It feels like every fibre in my body is alive when I'm touching him. Instead of pulling my hand away I continue touching him and notice that even though he doesn't turn his hand around to hold mine, he doesn't move his hand away. "I need to phone my parents to let them know that I am fine."

I see him frown at my request, but then he is stretching his leg and leaning back slightly as he tries to slide his phone out of his front jeans pocket. "Do you know the number?" I call out the number to him which he dials and then hands me the phone.

"Hello?" I hear my mother answer

"Mom."

"Oh, Anastasia, where have you been?" I hear what sounds like a gasp.

"I'm okay now Mom, I was kidnapped but I've been retrieved," I murmur yawning again, I can't believe that

ULRICH

I am tired again when I have just woken up from sleeping for one whole day.

"Oh, my word, are you hurt? Where are you?" I look at Ulrich as I talk to Mom and see that his attention is fully centred on me.

"I'm okay Mom, just really tired. How is Dad?" I murmur. My worry has been with how he is feeling as I always worry with his weak heart.

"He has been worried sick; we both have, but he's okay."

"I will phone you back tomorrow okay Mom," I want to talk longer to her, but my eyes don't seem to want to cooperate.

"But, where are you?" I don't really know, I'm about to ask Ulrich when he holds out his hand for the phone. When I frown, he nods. I reluctantly hand him the phone but only because I seem to have used up all the energy I had. Taking the phone he brings it to his ear.

"Hello," he says, and I hear my mom's voice saying something. "My name is Ulrich; the doctor was just here to check on your daughter and he assures us that she just needs to rest. I want you to know that she will be fine, we will take the best care of her." I close my eyes, as the conversation between Ulrich and Mom continues and no matter how much I want to carry on listening soon, I find myself dozing off.

I don't know how long I've been asleep for this time but when I wake up, I'm feeling so much more refreshed that I smile before opening my eyes, I feel a weight over my waist which has me looking down only to see an arm around my waist. Following the arm up to the body that is laying next to me I tense. Why is he sleeping with me? Instead of being upset at the audacity of him thinking he can just sleep with me I feel somewhat cherished which is silly as I don't even know the man.

Looking at his sleeping features I smile, his hair is falling over half of his face obscuring most of it to my view but I can still see the stubble that gives him such a manly naughty look, my fingers tingle at the thought of touching his jaw. His lashes are long and dark, his lips are plump and meant to be woken up with a kiss, but I don't dare.

I don't know how he can lay next to me; I must stink, and my hair must look like a rat's nest. Looking back down at my body I frown realizing for the first time that I am not wearing the dirty yellow dress that I had been wearing for such a long time, Instead I seem to be dressed in a white t-shirt. I look over at Ulrich again, wondering if he was the one to change me.

"I can feel you staring at me," he says in a gravely sleepy voice that sounds so sexy.

"Who changed my clothes?" His eyes open sleepily and then he grins, a cocky grin that I am sure has caught the attention of many women before.

"Don't worry I don't go in for ravishing women while they asleep." At his reply I feel a tinge of jealousy as I think of all the women this man must have ravished before, how could he ever want to even look at me when I must look like a scarecrow at the moment.

"I wasn't worried," I mutter.

"Liar," he murmurs as he raises his hand and tweaks my chin. I am stunned at the action as I can't remember when was the last time that anyone did that to me, I can't even remember my parents doing it. "It was the girls. When you arrived, they made sure you were comfortable before I arrived."

"What girls?" I see him frown and then he is lifting on his elbow as he looks down at me.

"Looks like you are feeling better," he says without answering my question which only makes me more curious. "Are you hungry, I will get someone to bring up something to eat." My stomach growls at the mention of food which has him grinning. "Well looks like the answer is yes," he says as he sits up, turning he leans forward and picks up his phone from the side table.

"Can I please have anything but bread with butter," I say feeling bad at being picky but after eating only two slices of bread with butter for days I think I can go awhile without eating any.

He looks over his shoulder at me, "don't you like bread or is it the butter?" he asks as he places the phone back on the side table after sending a text which I'm guessing is to ask for the food.

"Actually, I liked both, but after only eating two slices of stale bread with butter for days I can easily go a few days without eating any," I say only to see anger on his face.

"Assholes," he grunts, his muscles bunching on his back as he stands and then turns to face me again. Oh, man and I thought he was handsome when he had his t-shirt on, I can feel the heat rising at the perfection that is the male specimen before me. If anything good came out of this situation, it was meeting this man. If nothing more I will have memories of this hunk to keep me dreaming for many years to come. There is a wings tattoo across his chest with the words Elemental's MC, I also see the words from his shoulder blade down his bicep that says Family first. His left arm has the most beautiful tattoo, which I cannot really tell what it is, but the pattern has my eyes glued to it.

"I should have killed the fuckers." At the angry words, my thoughts snap back to the present, my eyes snapping up to his.

"What do you mean, what happened to them?" Are they going to come after me again? I can feel a knot growing in my stomach when I think of having to always look over my shoulder in fear.

"Nothing, they are detained. We need information from them on where they keep the women and how they transport them." At least they are detained, I start to push myself up so that I can sit up as my muscles are starting to ache from being in bed for such a long time but suddenly his hands are around my upper arms and he is helping me sit up.

"Umm, thank you," I murmur not used to having people helping me before he can say anything there is a knock at the bedroom door. He walks to the door, opening it I hear a feminine voice before I see the woman walk in. Ulrich inclines his head towards the bedside table and the woman approaches. There is a frown on her face as she looks at me. Who is she? As soon as she places the food on the bedside table, she is once again turning, her skin-tight jeans leaving little to the imagination and her tank top clearly shows her lack of a bra.

When I see Ulrich smiling at her, my anger rises which I know is unreasonable as I don't know him from anywhere and I must look a fright compared to the woman now standing before him simpering like a cat, her hand on his chest. "Do you need anything else?" she asks looking up at him, her fingers stroking their way up his chest.

"Not now, doll, you can leave," he says with a wink as he takes a step back. She pouts as she turns to head out the door. When he has closed the door, my anger is at fever pitch. I saw his eyes on her ass as she strolled out.

"You know, you don't have to stay here with me. Don't let me stop you from going about your business." I can hear the anger in my voice, and I know he can sense it too as his eyebrows rise in surprise.

"And now?" he asks as he frowns, but instead of answering I grunt in anger and turn to see what was brought up to eat. There is a plate that is covered, a glass with what looks like orange juice and something that is wrapped. I start to lean over to uncover the main plate but am stopped by Ulrich as he comes to stand by the plate. Looking back at him, I see him still looking at me with a frown.

"Why are you upset?" I know I am glaring as I look at him and I know that it is silly, I have no reason to be upset with the man, after all I barely know him, but the thought of him looking at another woman has me wanting to strangle him.

"I'm just hungry," I mutter and see his suspicious expression, but he turns, leaning down he uncovers the plate to show me scrambled eggs, the smell has my mouth watering. He then uncovers a plain croissant that looks perfectly flaky, like it will melt in my mouth. Placing the croissant on the plate next to the eggs, he picks up the plate and the fork and then he is sitting down next to me.

"What are you doing?" I ask as he brings the fork towards me, filled with egg.

"I'm feeding you," he says, I open my mouth to tell him that I can very well eat by myself when he places the egg in my mouth, instead of spluttering I close my mouth and chew, the taste of the egg after so long of not eating anything tasteful is like the best thing I have ever tasted. I lift my hand to take the fork away from him, but he moves his hand out of reach.

"I can feed mys. . ." again, he fills my mouth with egg when I try to argue with him.

"Mmmm, nice isn't it," he murmurs, and I can see a twinkle in his eye which has me glaring at him but instead of fighting him I decide to let him feed me if that makes him feel better, but if he thinks that I will always give in to his wishes, he has another think coming.

ULRICH 5

Anastasia falls asleep after me feeding her, which has me smiling when I think of her glare at my treating her like a baby, but the thought of feeding her was stronger than me. If she only knew how erotic I was finding it, every time she would take the egg off the fork into her mouth, her perky little tongue sometimes peeking out to lick a piece off her lip had me as hard as steel.

I have been in a state of arousal ever since I first saw her, but it has been getting worse with each day that passes. I can't pull myself away from her, it's like an obsession. I thought that I could fight our bond, I thought that I could delay the inevitable, but earlier when Tanya came in with the food and placed her hand on my chest all I wanted to do was push her away. The thought of sleeping with her or any other woman for that matter now completely unappetizing to me.

ULRICH

When I got back to the club and found her in my bed, it felt like everything fell into place. One of the Jezebels had given her a sponge bath while she was asleep, and even though she can still do with a proper bath, the dirt that was covering her body is mostly gone. I know that the longer I take to complete our bond the worse it will be, but I can't take her while she's still feeling weak. I saw the fire in her when I was feeding her and purposefully ignoring her attempt to feed herself. My woman seems to be a fighter but she will soon realize that I wear the pants in this relationship.

I listen to her breathing, her chest rising and falling with each breath she takes, her eyelashes dark against her pale skin. I frown as I hear a knock, Anastasia turns her head, but she doesn't awaken. I walk towards the door opening it quietly I see Tor. Stepping outside I close the door behind me, I don't want him inside the room, I find myself wanting no man near her. I have never been possessive, but now I find myself wanting Anastasia all to myself, especially where men are concerned.

"Tor" I greet, I haven't seen him since we came back from the docks. We didn't find out as much as we were expecting, but at least we stopped the shipment. There were another two women already in one of the containers, when we arrived there and the state that they were in was heart-breaking. At least Anastasia wasn't abused like those two women were, but the four men that were there are now in our basement together with the ones that we captured in the house and they will tell us everything they know before we get rid of them.

We also encountered Keres this time at the docks, he tried to escape when he sensed us but there was no escape and unfortunately we weren't able to capture him alive but we are getting closer and I am sure that soon we will know who is running this fucking trafficking ring.

"How is she?" he must have just had a shower earlier as his hair is still damp and I can smell the detergent on the clothes that he is wearing which tells me that he has changed into clean clothes and seeing as its late afternoon, he must have been out and come back not too long ago.

"She still spends most of her day sleeping, but the doctor said that she needs to recuperate and the best way to do it is sleep." Tor grunts at my comment as he lifts his hand to scratch at the stubble on his jaw.

"The other woman didn't make it." At Tor's comment I tense. Shit, it could have been Anastasia. We need to find the fuckers that think it's okay to do this to women.

"Shit, I hope she doesn't ask about her," I mutter, the last thing I want is to see sorrow in her eyes.

"How is it going with the two of you?" Tor asks, his eyes taking everything in.

"I'm getting to know her; she's still not well, I can't force our bond on her." To be honest, I don't know how long I can hold out. If I stay in this room with her for much longer, I won't be able to stop myself from making her completely mine.

"Do you know what her gift is yet?" Tor asks with a raised brow, I completely forgot about that, all the elemental mates have a specific gift, but until now I haven't seen anything that could indicate that Anastasia has any kind of gift. I shake my head in denial, I will have to somehow bring it up and see if she is willing to tell me when she doesn't even know me. I know from what I have heard from others that usually these women keep their gifts a secret as they are more times than none labelled freaks because of being different.

"Burkhart, Brandr and Bjarni are coming up sometime this week, they are bringing their women." I raise my brows in surprise.

"Why?"

"Let's just say that Brandr's woman can hear your thoughts." At his comment, I tense.

"No fucking way!" Why didn't anyone ever tell me that, I think back to any time that I might have been near her. I see Tor grin at my reaction as he slaps me not too gently on the arm.

"Make sure you are well and truly mated by the time

they get here; I want them to meet your woman and maybe help her with anything she might need in regard to her gift."

"Fuck Tor," I mutter, "you can't expect me to rush this."

"You should have been mated the minute you touched her, stop dragging your fucking feet and get it done." With those words, he turns and starts making his way down the corridor.

"It's not as simple as that you know," I mutter as I turn to enter the room once again.

"Of course, it is, you have been practicing enough for this your whole life so now show her how completely irresistible you are," I hear Tor say as he walks away. Closing the door behind me I look at Anastasia, I will ask one of the women to bring up clean towels and when she awakens, I will help her into the shower and help her shower. I smile when I think of the water running down her body, my fingers running over her perfect body. Seeing her wearing my t-shirt has me in a constant state of arousal, knowing that her naked body is rubbing against the same fabric that my body has rubbed has me wanting to walk up to her and rip that shirt off her body.

When I think about the docks and saw the drab container where she would have been taken it has my whole-body tensing. There wasn't even a blanket in there, they had a bucket in the corner for the women to relieve themselves like animals. We have Celmund looking into previous shipments and trying to find a link to this whole trafficking ring, but it seems like the company that is paying for the container is fictitious and we can't find any connection yet.

"You know, it's a little unsettling to wake up and have a man starring at you." Anastasia's words bring me back to the present to see her looking at me. I was so engrossed in my own thoughts that I didn't even realize that she had awoken.

"I was thinking that maybe you would like a shower," I say the first thing that comes to mind only to see her cheeks suddenly fill with colour. Maybe I'm not the only one that has been envisioning my hands stroking over her naked wet body. Damn, I better calm my thoughts or I'm going to pop the fastening on my jeans.

"Yes, I can just imagine how bad I must look." What? If she only knew what kind of a reaction, she is having on me, she wouldn't think that.

"You don't look bad," I mutter as I walk towards the side of the bed to help her up, as I lean forward to place my hands under her arms to pull her up, she tenses.

"What are you doing?" she asks with a shocked look on her face.

"I'm going to help you to the bathroom so that you can shower." I am starting to get the feeling that Anastasia doesn't let people help her much from her reactions. She doesn't reply but simply pushes herself up with my help. We soon have her on the side, her bare legs hanging from the side of the bed, the t-shirt riding high up her thighs. Instead of pulling her to her feet I lean down placing my one arm under her legs and the other around her back, I pick her up against my chest.

"Wait," I stop at her command. "Put me down I can walk." Instead of doing as she says I shake my head and make my way towards the bathroom. "You are really stubborn, aren't you," she mutters when I walk into the bathroom.

"No, you are the one being stubborn. You know it's much simpler for me to help you than having you stumbling around, maybe even injuring yourself."

"You know, when I chose you to help me over the other guy it didn't mean that you had to continue doing it. I don't want it to be a burden," she states as I lean forward to sit her on the edge of the bath.

"Trust me, you are no burden," I say as I step back from her to go and turn on the shower.

"Umm, can I maybe bath instead of shower?" What?

"I will help you in the shower," I mutter. At my comment I see her frown and then suddenly her cheeks darken with colour

"You are not showering with me," she mutters

"Why not?"

"What do you mean why not? I don't even know you."

"Well then this is the best way to get acquainted, wouldn't you say?" I reply with a wink, which seems to only infuriate her more.

"Look, I appreciate that you saved me from those guys and that you have looked after me while I have been down but I'm not going to sleep with you."

"I think you are still confused, I said shower, not sleep, and if you don't remember we have already slept together." At her glare I'm guessing I shouldn't have reminded her of that, well she will have to get used to it because I am expecting to sleep with her quite a lot and where showers are concerned, I think I will make it a habit of showering with her every day.

"I don't know what kind of women you are used to, but I'm not going to get naked with you." I raise a brow at her comment.

"You don't know this yet doll, but you are going to get naked with me and love every moment of it." I take a step towards her to pull up her t-shirt and encounter her hand up in the air as if to stop me, I nearly grin at this tiny little slip of a woman thinks that she can stop me.

"First of all, I'm not your doll, and secondly I am not going to get naked with you. You are really conceited, aren't you?"

I shrug as I take another step towards her, my chest against her flat palm. Leaning forward I take hold of her t-shirts and start to tug only to feel a blast of cold against my chest, "What the hell?" standing up straight I look down at my chest, lifting my hand I touch my chest feeling the coolness of my skin and then I smile, the smile turning into a grin and finally a chuckle. This is just too perfect; my woman is ice to my fire.

"I am about to melt all that ice into a puddle," I say with a grin as I raise my hand imagining a flame, the flame starts small and then grows in my hand until it covers the palm. I see her mouth open in surprise, her eyes open wide as they look up at me from my hand.

"How are you doing that?" she asks

"The same way as you tried to freeze me, only problem vixen is that I'm too hot to be frozen." She raises her hand towards the flame, and I know that she is trying to see if it's a figment of her imagination, but when she feels the heat, she retracts her hand.

"Show me what you can do," I say as I close my hand to extinguish the flame. She shakes her head as she pulls her hands besides her on the side of the bath. "Why not?" I ask with a frown; I want her to show me everything that she can do.

"Since being taken that I wasn't able to do anything, this is the first time that I managed to use my gift since the kidnapping," she murmurs.

"Well it will grow stronger, especially now that you are with me." I see her frown at my statement but I don't elaborate as I move in the blink of an eye and pull the t-shirt up and over her head, because she wasn't expecting it her arms went up easily facilitating the removal of it.

"Aargh" she screams, "What the hell?" one of her hands is trying to cover her beautifully rounded breasts while the other has gone down to cover her mound. I could just kiss her whole body right now and to hell with all of this.

"Enough talk, time to shower," I state only to see her glaring at me.

"I am not showering with you," she states.

"You can't shower alone yet, so yes, you will be showering with me, but don't worry I know you will enjoy it." My hand goes to the button of my jeans and I see her eyes snap closed.

"Don't you dare do this Ulrich," she says angrily but I don't listen as I drop my jeans on the ground and then I am leaning into the shower to turn the water on, when I turn back to Anastasia I see her looking at me, her eyes traveling over my body.

"Like what you see?" I say as I turn towards her only to see her cheeks darken with colour, her teeth biting her lower lip unconsciously, my cock pulsing with need at her perusal. I have never wanted a woman as much as I want Anastasia at this very moment without a second thought I have her face between my hands, my head lowering as I take her lips in a passionate kiss.

ANASTASIA 6

His touch takes me by surprise and then the kiss has just blown my mind, I have been kissed before, but I have never been kissed like this before. My whole body feels alive, as if I can feel the blood coursing right under my skin. It doesn't help that he is drop dead gorgeous or that he has a body that would make Adonis weep with envy.

I pull the arm that is between the two of us covering my breasts up until the palm is flat against his rock-hard chest, feeling the movement of the muscle under my fingers, the smoothness of his skin warm to the touch. I don't know why this man affects me the way he does, his simple look has my body on fire. He is overbearing and demanding something that I have never liked before but with this man every time I have argued with him it has felt like a sexual play of words that has my body ringing with passion.

"You are mine," he mutters as he lowers his head from my lips to my neck

"No," I murmur, as his lips kiss my neck, the junction between my collar bone and neck sensitive to his touch as my skin rises in Goosebumps at his touch. Suddenly I feel myself being lifted, opening my eyes I see Ulrich stepping into the shower, the warm water splashing me as he slides me down his body until my feet are touching the ground once again. The warm water now sliding over my body, soothing the aches and pains that my body is still trying to heal.

I have craved bathing; it is strange the things we miss when we don't have them any longer, but now under this shower there is nothing like I crave more than this man that is standing beside me. I see his hand move towards the dispenser before me and squeeze out some shower gel onto his hand, the warmth of his fingers over my skin lathering my body with soap has me closing my eyes in pleasure.

He then pulls a container down from a shelf and pours some liquid into his hand. When I feel his fingers in my hair, I tense waiting for the pain. The knots in my hair will be difficult to untangle after so long without washing it, but to my surprise I feel no pain, instead his fingers massage my sculp gently relaxing every fibre of my being.

"Mmmm," I murmur in pleasure and hear him grunt as I lean my head back.

"You like this?" his voice is gruff; I can hardly understand what he said, so instead of answering I nod. He turns me gently and then the water is washing away the shampoo.

"This shampoo smells so good," I murmur, loving the gentle scent of spice that is wafting around me. I open my eyes only to see Ulrich looking down at me with an intensity that has my breath catching. His hair is wet, the water running in rivulets down his chest. His eyes seem to be boring into my very soul.

"Can you feel it?" he asks as I see his head lowering, I'm feeling lots of things but I'm not sure what he is referring to, so I don't reply. "Can you feel this between us?"

As I open my mouth to reply he swoops down and takes my lips in a blistering kiss that has me wanting more. My arms rise to hook around his neck, his tongue playing his love tune with mine, bringing me to a state of heightened passion like I have never been before. His hands are under my ass and he is lifting me, I feel him shifting and then we are walking out of the shower, the next thing I know I am being laid down on the bed.

"The bed is going to get wet," I murmur as he moves over me, instead of answering he grunts but doesn't lift me again instead his lips are on my neck and he is kissing me like a man possessed. He has a hand on either side of my torso, his fingers fanned out covering my whole torso, showing me his strength as he suddenly pulls me slightly down, his eyes now in line with mine.

"I want you," his words are gruff his eyes intense as he looks at me and I know that if I want to stop this, now is the time to say so. I open my mouth to tell him that maybe we shouldn't do this now.

"I want you too." Where the hell did that come from? Before I can retract what I said, his lips are over mine and he is kissing me with a passion that has my whole-body tingling. I don't know what it is about him, but he has me feeling like I have never felt before. I have slept with other men before, in my twenty-six years it would be strange If I hadn't, but none of them blew my mind like he does, maybe it's because my system is still run down from being kidnapped and the lack of nutrients in my diet.

Every thought disappears from my mind when his hands push my breasts together and his lips are kissing them, his teeth nipping gently at my nipples, which has me gasping in pleasure at the feeling. I lower my hand to his head, entwining my fingers in his hair I hold his head closer to me wanting this feeling to last as long as I can have it.

His hands let go of my breasts and start making their way down my body, his body sliding down kissing every inch of my stomach, my navel, his hand slides under my ass as he lifts it up from the bed kissing his way between my legs.

"Ulrich, ohhhh," I murmur as I feel the smoothness of his tongue flickering between my legs, lapping at my womanhood. My hands at his shoulders, feeling the muscles under my fingers, his body warm to my cool touch. I feel my whole body start to tighten as I feel myself orgasming at his ministrations, my eyes close as I throw my head back groaning in pleasure as I let go of all inhibitions or all thought and let myself find the pleasure that this man is giving me.

I am still coming down from my high when I feel him entering me, he penetrates my body slowly as he stretches me to accommodate his size. His elbows next to my body as dips his head to my shoulder, his movements at first slow as he kisses me, "you are perfect," he mutters against my ear as his movements quicken, building up the passion once again. A feeling of fulness, of extreme pressure building in my body making me delirious with want and then just when I think that it can't get any better, just when my body starts to tighten once again I feel pain in my shoulder which has my orgasm exploding all around him, my mind feels like it's floating.

My hand lifts to his neck and I grab the black leather chain that he is wearing, the beautiful amber that is hanging from it scorching to the touch, and then I hear his beautiful words in my ear. "I join us forever and always, where one goes the other shall follow. I will hold you above everyone and everything else. I will protect you until my last breath. My body, my soul and mind are forever yours and yours is mine." And then I hear him roar in release and something moist trickles into my mouth. Opening my eyes, I see his wrist over my mouth, his head thrown back in the throes of his release, a gash on his wrist that is bleeding.

I gasp when I realize that I must have bitten his wrist, reaction from the force of my release. It must have been his blood I tasted in my mouth, lifting my hand I place it over his gash feeling terrible that I hurt him even if unintentionally.

My body still vibrating with pleasure, I once again close my eyes to enjoy every moment of this encounter. I don't know if this experience was this wild because of my debilitated state or because Ulrich is definitely the best-looking man, I have ever been with or the fact that he can drive me wild with his stubbornness. Whatever the reason for what happened, I want to enjoy it to its very last second.

I must have fallen asleep, because the next thing I know I am shooting up in pain as I feel my shoulder blade burning as if on fire. "What's wrong?" Ulrich asks as he too sits up in bed looking at me.

"My shoulder is burning, like its on fire. Is this your doing?" Ulrich leans back to look at my shoulder and I feel him tensing around me.

"It will be fine in a minute," I feel his lips lightly on my skin which has me gasping in pain, he then blows on my back. "I'm sorry," he murmurs which has me tensing.

"For what?"

"The tattoo that is appearing on your shoulder blade, the tattoo that proves you are mine." At his words I snap away from his hands and turn staring at him.

"What, what do you mean?"

"You are mine as such you will get a tattoo like the one I have on my arm, that tattoo has just started to appear on your arm?" Is he joking? I try to look over my shoulder but cant see anything, how can a tattoo just appear? Wait, he did this while I was sleeping?

"How dare you tattoo me while I'm asleep?" I can't believe the audacity of the man, "I'm not a piece of meat that you can brand."

"The tattoo is more like a birth mark and it is unavoidable, it is linked to what will keep you safe." How can he think to make this decision for me, this is my body and a tattoo isn't exactly something that I can just ignore.

"You have no right to make decisions like that for me," I feel myself glaring at him but at the moment I don't like him too much.

"Look, there is nothing I can do about it. You have a gift and so do I, when you join two people like us the tattoo appears." Is he saying that he didn't do the tattoo, that it was done because of our gifts? There is a knock on the door. "Go back to sleep, it's just Dag," he murmurs and walks towards the door naked. How does he know who it is if he hasn't opened the door yet, and who is Dag?

He opens the door a crack, "what's up?"

"I sent you a text three hours ago," I hear the man say

"So, what are you, my wife?" Ulrich mutters, which has me immediately wondering if he is in fact married. Oh, please tell me that I didn't sleep with a married man. "I was busy," Ulrich states

"Sorry to disturb your beauty sleep, but if you had read the text, then I wouldn't have to come and call you." I can hear the man's sarcasm in the tone of his voice, "We got another tip, we are leaving in the morning. Tor said you will stay here with Colborn and Asger."

"Fine, is that it?"

"Draco and some of his men are arriving tomorrow."

"What? Tor said Bjarni, Brandr and Burkhart he didn't

say Draco was coming." By Ulrich's irritated reply, it sounds like he's not too keen on Draco's visit.

"Well he is, he heard you had found your mate, so he wants to meet her." I see Ulrich tense, what does the guy mean when he says that Ulrich has found his mate?

"Fine, I'll be down before you guys leave." With those words Ulrich closes the door, my eyes traveling over his impressive naked body as he turns towards me.

"Who's Draco?" I ask as Ulrich draws his fingers through his hair.

"Draco is the whole of the Elemental's MC President, Tor that you will meet sometime is the Cape Town chapter president," he replies as he walks towards the bed.

"Why don't you like him?" I ask frowning when I see Ulrich's look of surprise.

"Who said I don't like Draco?"

"You didn't seem very happy when Dag mentioned that Draco was going to be here tomorrow," I state as he sits on the side of the bed, I pull the sheet tighter around me now embarrassed to have this man see my nakedness.

"That wasn't me not liking Draco, I have the highest respect for him. He has been with me in fights many times and I would consider myself privileged to have him at my back in a fight any day. It's just that Tor and Draco are quite different, even though they are the best of friends they disagree on most things." He places his hand on my sheet covered calf, stroking it with his thumb.

"You will see when you meet both of them, they are both forces to be reckoned with, the only difference is that we don't always follow instruction too well and Draco does not like unruliness." I smile as I look at him, I can't imagine this man being anything else but unruly. His whole demeanor screams it. Now for the question that I am dreading.

"Are you married?" At my question he tenses, his eyes snapping up from my neck to my eyes.

"What the hell gave you that idea?" he asks.

"Dag said Draco wants to meet your mate, who is your mate then and why call her your mate?" Ulrich mutters something under his breath which I don't understand and then he is standing up, walking towards a set of draws he opens one and pulls out jeans that he proceeds to slide up his muscular legs.

"You are," he finally replies as he turns towards me, a dark golden yellow t-shirt nearly the colour of his stone in his hand.

"What do you mean?" I ask as he slips the t-shirt on, the fabric stretching across his ripped chest and muscular arms.

"I mean that you are mine, remember when I showed you my fire and you can manifest cold." I frown, what does that have to do with anything.

"I don't see how that has got to do with anything, and I'm not yours, this here," I point towards the bed twisting my finger around in a circle, "was just a one-time thing, this didn't mean anything." I am such a liar, even as I say it I know that it is not true, I have never before felt like I am feeling right now or like I felt when this man that is standing before me with a scowl that would make a weaker person run, touched me with a passion that had me completely and utterly overwhelmed.

His hands are now low on his waist, his eyes boring into me, "I have news for you Vixen, this here is far from over." He then points at me, "you might not know it yet, but you are mine and nothing anyone does can ever change that." I sit up straight in bed, my anger rising at his presumptuousness seeing him bend down as he ties the laces on his boots.

"That's what you think, I will not be anyone's toy." He stands up straight from tying his boots and then he is walking towards the door, opening the door he looks back at me.

"You are wrong, you will be my toy and you will love it." With those words, he is stepping out and closing the door behind him.

"No, I won't," I grab the pillow from next to me and throw it at the door, "Aargh," I mutter angrily. How dare he just leave. If he thinks that I am going to be here at his beck and call just because he saved me from the kidnappers, then he has another think coming. The minute I am feeling better I will be out of here and then I want to see what Mr. high and mighty is going to do.

ULRICH 7

"Didn't expect you down now," Dag says as he sits back drinking coffee, his legs stretched out before him, everything is silent as it's still pitch dark outside and not morning yet.

"Well I didn't expect you to wake me up in the early hours but guess what you did," I mutter as I pull forward a chair and sit next to him.

"You don't sound in the throes of bliss like I hear newly mated couples are," Dag states as he lifts a black brow over his piercing blue eyes.

"It was fine until you opened your big mouth," I mutter as I cross my arms, it's unfair to blame Dag as sooner or later I would have had to tell Anastasia but at the moment it feels good to blame someone.

"Me?" he asks with a surprised look, "what the hell did I say?"

"She didn't know that she was my mate, she asked me if I was married at what you asked so I had to tell her." I raise my hands to rub in frustration at my face, I have never had a problem with turning my back on a woman and walking out but now for some reason I just want to go back and make sure that she isn't upset, damn, this bonding is a problem but I knew it was going to be a problem.

"I guess she doesn't want you as a mate," at his words I drop my hands and glare at him.

"There is nothing wrong with me being a mate," I snap, he shrugs and takes another sip of his coffee. "She will come around." I hope it happens soon, but Anastasia seems like the type of person that doesn't like to be coerced into situations. What if she doesn't want to stay with me?

"I thought you didn't want a mate," Dag says suddenly as he lowers his mug.

"I didn't, but it's true what they say, the pull is irresistible." The thought of Anastasia leaving has my anger rising, my stomach knotting and my mind ready to find and kill anyone that helps her leave. "She's Mine," I state, the possessiveness that I feel for that woman upstairs in my room is something that I have never felt before in my life for anyone or anything.

"So, I see," Dag says with a smile as he sits forward and then slaps me on the back. "Stop fighting it Bro, you have been given a beautiful woman as a mate, where is that Ulrich charm that you always bragging about? Go and show her that she can't be without you." At his words I frown, I don't think that Anastasia is the type to be swayed by a smile, but I'm not the sweet words poet type, so she will have to accept me for the coarse, unruly man that I am.

"She's argumentative," I mutter

"Well, that's going to be interesting then because you are one argumentative son of a bitch, I can't wait to see your woman put you in your place." That has me scowling at him just as Haldor walks in, Monica walking next to him with a grumpy look on her face. Haldor doesn't like anyone messing with his stuff so I can imagine that he wouldn't want Monica in his room if he has to leave. Guess he kicked her out of bed.

"Man, you can see that things have changed," he says as he comes to stand before us, Monica has gone to the bar to make him a coffee.

"Sweetheart bring me one too," I call out to her and see

her smile over her shoulder at me as she nods. "What has changed?" I then ask as I look at Haldor and realize I shouldn't have asked as I see him grinning.

"Well, you are one of the first of us down today must be the company you are keeping. Usually we have to drag your ass out of bed." I lift my hand to show him the finger, which has Dag and him laughing. "Doesn't say much for this mating does it?" Haldor teases which has me glaring at him

"There is nothing wrong with my bond," I mutter.

"I think he's sounding a bit defensive; don't you think Dag?" Haldor quips just as Monica hands me the cup of coffee and then slides onto my lap. I grunt but don't tell her to stand even though her nearness has me feeling agitated. I have always loved women around me, giving women attention, but now that I have my mate, I feel myself feeling repelled by this woman's nearness. I bring the mug to my mouth as I take a sip, I see Dag raise an eyebrow at Monica, but he doesn't say anything.

"Oh, ahh…" Haldor says suddenly looking a bit flustered, "should you be out of bed?" At his words my whole-body tenses, fuck, I glance over my shoulder only to see Anastasia standing in the doorway her hand holding onto the doorframe. A scowl on her face, oh fuck, she looks furious and I'm sure that I am just about to hear exactly what she thinks when she looks at Haldor.

I push at Monica to get up and hear her mutter of displeasure, but she stands walking towards Dag. Anastasia looks at Haldor and then I see her eyes widen slightly as I stand. "It's you, the handsome one. You never introduced yourself." At her comment I feel anger rise up as I turn to look at Haldor, I see him smile at her which is his biggest mistake, pulling back my arm I throw a punch hitting him on the side of his cheek. That will mess up his handsomeness for a while, I want to see what she thinks of him like that.

"What the hell?" I hear Haldor mutter, at the same time as Anastasia shrieks in anger.

"You Caveman." One minute she is by the door and the next she is making her way towards Haldor that is looking ready to attack me. I swear if she touches him, he is dead, I feel my vision sharpening my whole body tensing ready to fight. She is mine and I will be damned if she touches one of my brothers. Deep down I know that Haldor is doing nothing, but to know that she thinks him handsome has every fibre in my body on alert.

Just before she reaches Haldor I slide my arms around her waist lifting her off the floor, "what the hell do you think you are doing, put me down," she says angrily, her legs and arms flailing uselessly as no matter how much she fights there is no way that I am going to place her on the floor to go to Haldor. "Put me down, how dare you. Go play with your other toy, I'm not one of your collection."

"She's not my toy," I mutter against her ear as I start making my way towards the door, I'm going to carry her back to the room, kicking and screaming if I have to but she is not going to stay anywhere near Haldor.

"Really, I'm not blind," she says angrily as she pulls her hand back to elbow me in the ribs but her measly attempt at getting free would never overpower me.

"Problems, already?" Dane asks as he walks towards us, but I don't answer as I continue making our way towards the room.

"Be still," I mutter but that only fuels her anger which has her wiggling around like an eel, and then suddenly she just goes completely still. "Anastasia?" I call but she doesn't answer, "are you okay?" entering the room I hurry towards the bed, placing her on it gently. Just as I step back, she springs up and glares at me. "Who do you think you are?" she says angrily, her eyes intense with her anger.

"I don't want to see you anywhere near Haldor, do you hear me?" At my words she stands, her finger pointing at me.

"Don't you dare tell me what I can and cannot do, I'm not your property."

"That's where you are wrong, you are mine and I won't

have you looking at any of my brothers." The fury coursing through my body at the thought that she finds Haldor attractive has me wanting to commit murder.

"That's rich coming from you, what do you think this is? I saw you with a woman on your lap and you are telling me that I can't find someone attractive. Well I hate to tell you this but we are in the twentieth century buster and what is good for the goose is good for the gander." She takes a step closer to me now, if she only knew how close I am to showing her just how much she belongs to me she would keep well away from me. Besides, we had sex once, it's not as if we married."

Those words snap my control. She thinks that all we did was have sex. I didn't want this bond in the first place, but now she is mine and I will be damned if she thinks that she can carry on acting single. Well I will show her how wrong she is, she will have no doubt in her mind who she belongs to and she will never doubt it again.

One minute I am standing by the door and the next I have her flat on her back on the bed, only now realizing that all she was wearing downstairs was my t-shirt. "You will never walk in front of my brothers like this, what the fuck, you are nearly naked."

"Oh please, I have more clothes on than your dear friend had." At the mention of Monica again I lower my head taking her lips in a blistering kiss, but she fights me only fuelling my anger more. She turns her head, but I raise my hand and turn her head back and then my lips are kissing her in an intense, no-nonsense way. Her hands try to push me away, but I don't budge and continue kissing her until she finally runs out of steam, she's not kissing me back but she's not pushing me away either.

I don't know how long I kiss her for but we are both breathless when I finally lift my head as I move to her neck kissing her just behind her ear, my hand has made its way under the t-shirt and is now stroking her nipple.

She's not participating, but she's not fighting it either, I can tell by the reaction of her body that she's enjoying my touch, but she is fighting it. My other hand moves between her legs, stroking over her panties. At first, she closes her legs which has me moving my body between her legs to keep them open and then I am slipping the panties to the side as I slip my finger between her folds. Suddenly she is pushing at me again, her hands at my shoulders.

"You will not touch me after you have just been touching another woman," she says angrily.

"I was not touching her," I state as I lift my head and look her in the eye.

"Monica was making coffee, when she brought mine, she sat on my lap, that is it." I state.

"That is, it? Really, " she says, "does that mean that you

have women sitting on your lap a lot." Her tone is sarcastic as she glares at me.

"You are my mate, the only woman now for me," I state and see the look of disbelief on her face as she glares at me.

"I'm not your mate, and you lie," she snaps, "I would just have to turn around and you would have someone else. I will not sleep with someone that can't keep it in his pants." I bring my fist down on the bed angrily. This woman can frustrate me like no one has ever been able to do.

"I will never lie to you; you are my mate and as such you are my other half. I wouldn't be able to touch another woman even if I wanted to. That is just how we Elemental's are." I sit back on my haunches, looking down at her. "Once we find our mate, that is it, you are the only woman for me, and I will be the only man for you."

She grunts as she turns her head away irritatingly which has me leaning forward and once again taking hold of her jaw with my hand and turning her head until she is once again facing me. "Do you understand me?"

"Do all your women believe in this story? Because I will tell you now that I don't believe one word that you are saying and as soon as I can, I will be out of here." The thought of her out there alone has my heart feeling as if it is being squeezed.

"There are no more women, and you belong with me," I state as I let go of her jaw and get up off the bed, "You don't understand yet what I am saying but you will see that what I say is true, you will feel the pull as much as I do and you will realize that we need to be together because we are meant to be." I am standing next to the bed, my hands low on my waist as I look down at her.

"Besides, you can't leave as the men that had you will be looking for you. They want every woman that has a gift and they won't give up if you are unprotected again." She sits up, her arms crossing over her chest as she looks up at me.

"What's the difference, it seems that I'm just as locked up here," she says angrily, which has me throwing my hands up in irritation.

"Does it look like you are locked up? You haven't been well woman, what did you want us to do?" With those words I turn and make my way towards the door, "I suggest you rest, and when you wake up you can come to the front and get breakfast, you will see that we are not keeping you locked up." I walk out closing the door behind me, this woman can ignite my anger like no one else can but she does the same with everything, my passion for her is blazing but I will not fight with her any longer today.

She will realize that what I say is true, and that she is mine. Making my way to the bar I find most of the men there already. When I enter, they all look around at me, the question in everyone's mind evident. "What the fuck was that for?" Haldor asks as I approach.

"I don't want you anywhere near my woman," I state, I know that I am being unreasonable but knowing that Anastasia finds him attractive has my anger ready to explode.

"I don't want your woman, it's not my fucking fault that she thinks I'm handsome." I glare at his statement taking a step closer to him, I know that Haldor would never try anything with my mate, but my possessiveness is riding me.

"Enough," Tor says as he walks towards both of us, "we have never had a fight among us because of a woman and we are not going to start now." He looks directly at me as he continues, "do you understand Ulrich? Sort your shit out and then I want peace among you." I nod, because I know that he is right, but I have never felt like this about anyone. I knew that finding my mate would be a problem, I didn't want this but now I will kill anyone that threatens to take it away.

ANASTASIA 8

How can I believe him when I saw that woman sitting on his lap? The anger that filled every fibre of my being at seeing his betrayal was all consuming. I know that we only had sex but for some reason I feel like he is mine and I have never been one to take abuse sitting down. Is it possible that what he said is true? I shake my head at the thought, I'm deluding myself if I believe him. He said that I am his mate but just after sleeping with me he has a woman sitting on his lap. How can it be true?

My anger is still pumping through my body every time I think of what I saw, and how dare he punch Haldor when he is the one that was in the wrong. I confess that I saw the opportunity to take a dig at him and took it, but I never thought that he would retaliate by punching Haldor. I didn't lie when I said that Haldor is handsome, but so are all the others that I saw. I will never confess to him that to me he is the better looking of all of them, and his charisma has me hot and bothered when he is close.

I don't know if what he said is true, I don't know if those men are still looking for me, but I know that I don't want them to get hold of me again. I will have to one way or another go back to my life, but how am I going to do that when in reality I want to stay here. I know that this is a fantasy and that I will need to go back to my life sooner or later, my parents will be missing me, and I can just imagine how Mr. Smith is doing without me.

I need to get hold of Mr. Smith, let him know that I will be coming back soon, but every time I think of phoning him I hesitate as it becomes too real the fact that I will have to leave soon and for some reason Ulrich has a hold on me that no one else has been able to do before. I don't know if what he says is true and there is some kind of bond between us, but I know that I find it more and more difficult to be away from the man when he isn't near. My mind is continuously on him, when he is away, I want him close and when he is close, he vexes me to the point of violence.

I wonder if I go look for Ulrich if he has another woman in his presence, I lift my hand to my hair and groan when I feel the curls in disarray. I'm going to have to wash my hair again so that I can tame my curls, and then I will try to find something to wear before I go out again. I want to see if what he said is true and if anyone tries to stop me when I'm not in the room.

My body is still slightly lethargic, but I need to get out of here and do something because I can't sit in this room for another hour with nothing to do. I make my way to the bathroom and turn on the water in the shower. The water is hot and soothing. My hand moves to my neck where I saw the bruise earlier on. I have a vague recollection of Ulrich biting me there, the thought still has my body tingling. After washing my hair, I make my way out of the shower, drying my body as I walk towards the room just as I hear a knock on the door.

Wrapping the towel around myself I walk to the door, opening it I encounter a woman standing on the other side, her black hair long, her tight black dress like a second skin. "Hi," I say seeing her eyes move over my body, my face and then my wet hair.

"Ulrich asked that I bring you these," I look down at her hand to find a pair of jeans and two t-shirts neatly folded. "It should fit, you're not as skinny as me but those are loose." I look down at her clothes.

"Thank you so much."

"No need, Ulrich will pay me back," she says as she turns and walks away. At her comment I want to throw the clothes at her back, pay her back indeed. I will wear these clothes because I want to leave the room, but I sure as hell won't have Ulrich owe the woman any favours, especially the way she suggested he was going to pay her back. I close the door to the room and quickly pull the jeans on and then the t-shirt. I don't have a bra, so, unfortunately; I will have to go without one, but desperate times call for desperate measures.

I pass my fingers through my hair trying to take the nots out but to no avail. Looking around, I don't see a brush, walking back into the bathroom I open the cabinet under the sink to find a brush but there is none. I am about to walk back into the room when I see a comb near one of the towel racks. Picking it up I start the cumbersome job of taking the knots out of my hair, I walk to the room, sitting on the bed I take piece by piece of hair until I have taken all the knots out and then I shake my head feeling the curls pop up around my head.

I finally feel like myself again, I take strands of hair and pull it back from my face, I don't have shoes but I'm not planning on going outside so for now this will have to do. I open the door and make my way once again down the corridor and then down the stairs to where I can hear talking. For now, I just want to find some food as my stomach has started to rumble with hunger.

"I see that you are feeling better and looking better too." At the sound of the man's voice, I jump in surprise as I didn't see anyone when I stepped off the bottom step.

"Oh, you startled me," I say looking at the man that is standing against the frame of a door just to my back. "Yes, much better thank you," I say smiling at his watchful look, like all the other men this one is also handsome but there is a sadness in his eyes that pulls at my heart. He has dark brown hair, cut short that shows off his strong jaw and tanned features. I can see a tattoo on his neck and his arms are covered in them. This man has a look about him that gives him an air of being haunted. All I want to do is go up to him and hug him tight.

"I'm Eirik," he says as he moves away from the door and approaches me, "I'm guessing you're looking for Ulrich?" At his question I shake my head.

"No, actually I'm looking for food." At my reply he smiles, but I notice that the smile doesn't reach his eyes.

"Food over Ulrich?" he quips, "he will never live that down."

"I'm sure he will be fine; his ego is inflated enough to last him a lifetime," I mutter and this time I get Eirik to grin.

"Well then Anastasia, follow me and I will lead you to food," he says as he walks past me, down the corridor but instead of turning to where the noise of voices is coming, he continues until we enter a spacious kitchen. There is a woman sitting on the kitchen counter with a bowl in her hand eating what looks like cereal.

"Camille, get off the counter," Eirik mutters as he shakes his head at her. She doesn't say anything, just uncrosses her legs and slides down and off the counter, her noticeably short shorts riding up her ass. She looks at me, her eyes traveling over my body and then face.

"Who are you?" she asks.

"I'm Anastasia," I reply and get a nod before she looks back down at her cereal, what a weird bunch.

"You can help yourself to anything you like, the food cupboards are there," Eirik says pointing to one side of the kitchen where the cupboards run the length of the kitchen, "and everything else is in the fridge."

"Thank you, I will have a look."

"Anastasia, if you need anything just let one of us know and we will get it for you." That is so sweet of him, but I must say that all the men I have met here have been nice, except for Ulrich that just irritates me.

"Thank you Eirik, that is really kind of you, but I think I'll just have some cereal," I say as I walk towards the fridge to find the milk. I see Camille approaching Eirik, she places her hand on his chest as she looks up at him her other hand still holding the bowl with cereal.

"I saw a sexy dress that would look really great on me, would you get it for me?" her voice is nasally as she tries to sound sexy.

"Didn't Tor pay you this month?" Eirik asks with a raised brow as he looks down at her

"Yes," she says with a frown.

"Well then, I'm sure you can buy it yourself." I have to force myself not to grin at his reply as I grab the box of cereal and look down to place some in my bowl.

"But you just said to her that she can ask for anything she wants." Camille whines as she glares at me, "what is so special about her?" I hear Eirik grunt in annoyance as he steps away from her touch.

"She's Ulrich's Old lady," Eirik mutters as he makes his way out of the kitchen.

"What?" Camille says in surprise as she turns to look at me, "Ulrich got himself an old lady?" I know that the bikers call their women old ladies, I had never thought in my wildest dreams that I would one day be called someone's old lady but here I am without even quite knowing how I got to this point, I'm someone's old lady.

"How did you get him to make you his old lady?" Camille asks with a frown as she now stands looking at me as Eirik decided to leave without answering her. I shrug as I bring a spoon of cereal to my mouth. Even if I wanted to answer her, I wouldn't know what to say. "There are no old ladies here, and out of all of them Ulrich would have been the last one that I would have thought would get an old lady." I'm sure he is, and she seems disgruntled that she wasn't the one chosen.

Well, now that she has mentioned that there are no old ladies here, it is easy to deduce that the women that I have seen until now are not with any of the men but give their favours to whoever catches their fancy. In general, I don't have a problem with it, but I do have a problem if Ulrich is one of the men that they are sleeping with.

"Eirik said you were here." I turn to see Ulrich walking in, his eyes rove over my face and then body I see what looks like appreciation light his eyes but I'm not sure.

"You got yourself an Old Lady?" Camille asks as she turns to him, I see his eyebrows rise at her question. "Why, you didn't need one." At her statement his expression turns into a frown.

"Yes, I did, and you will respect her as such. Do you understand me?" I can see the surprise on her face at his snapped reply, she nods. Placing her bowl on the counter she turns and leaves.

"You know, I'm not your old lady," I say when she's gone.

"Don't start," he mutters, "when you're done, I'll introduce you to the others." I could argue, but I'm also tired of the constant bickering, so I don't say anything as I continue eating until I'm finished and then I walk towards the sink. Rinsing off my bowl, I place it on the drying rack before turning towards him again to find his eyes on my body.

"You are beautiful." His words have me stopping in surprise.

"And you are a sweet talker," I mutter embarrassed at the compliment.

"No, I'm telling you the truth." He steps towards me, his hand raises to my cheek, the other one moves towards my hair. He grabs a curl pulling it straight and then letting it go which immediately has the curl bouncing back into place. He smiles as his eyes clash with mine, "I could look at you the whole day."

"Now that would be freaky," I mutter trying to hide my awkwardness as I have never been one to take compliments easily. Everyone takes me for an independent, strong woman and I am those, but I am also an awkward, uncertain woman when men compliment me. His lips touch mine gently and then he is kissing me, this kiss is different from the others, this kiss is gentle and soft giving me the choice to step back if I want to instead of his previous overpowering kisses.

When he lifts his head, we are both flushed with

passion, my heart racing, my body tingling. I don't know what he does to me but whatever it is, it's explosive. One kiss from this man and my heart is racing, my mind is in chaos and all I want to do is kiss him again. "Come, let me introduce you to the others before they leave."

He takes hold of my hand and then he is walking towards the door, guiding me down the corridor and towards where I can hear men's voices. Entering the bar area, we stop my eyes traveling over everyone there, darn there is a man for every woman's fantasy here. They are all using Kutts like Ulrich's and short sleeve t-shirts that leaves their arms bare. I notice that most of them have both arms tattooed, and only a couple with one arm tattooed. They are all muscular, tall, and at the moment every single one of them is looking at me.

"This is Anastasia," Ulrich says as he lets go of my hand and places his arm around my shoulders, he takes a step forward pulling me with him. A tall daredevil of a man steps forward and I swear if I didn't know better, I would say that I was transported back in time. His hair is a long honey blond, loose around his shoulders with thin plaits on either side of his head. His eyes, a magnetic blue as he looks at me, there is a gold armband around his right forceps confirming the look of Viking that he has going.

"Welcome Anastasia, you are truly a diamond among gems." And a flirt. His smile lights up his eyes, but the words and smile don't detract from the fact that this man is dangerous. There is an aura of danger that surrounds him, I feel like at any moment he will snap and then all hell will break loose.

"This is Tor and our President." Even without telling me that he's the president I would have guessed as his very presence shouts out authority.

"Nice to meet you." I say with a smile, but inside I feel knots in my stomach at being surrounded by so many dangerous men.

"You have met Eirik," Ulrich says as he points a finger at Eirik that is standing to one side, "Eirik is our Sargent at Arms." I smile at Eirik as he nods at me. "Over there you have Tal" I look at the man standing next to Eirik seeing a man with long dark brown hair up in a bun, his dark brown eyes twinkling as if he is keeping a secret.

"I'm Dane, he's taking way too long to get to me." A man on the other side of the group says, turning my head I see a big mountain of a man, hair to his shoulders, square jaw, but the most amazing thing about this man is his mismatched eyes, one is a dark blue and the other a light green. His tan has his eyes more visible.

"Yes, he's a bit slow," I murmur which has the men burst out laughing.

"Fuck brother, your woman has you all figured out already," Tor states with a grin.

"I'll have to show her that she's wrong," Ulrich says with a wink and a naughty grin that has me shaking my head at his silliness.

"Ignore him, he doesn't know how to treat a lady." A man standing to Ulrich's left says, "I'm Calborn, and if you need me to knock some sense into him sometime, just let me know."

I grin at him, "I think you are going to be very busy Colborn." At my quip Colborn lifts his hands in a boxing pose which has the men laugh.

"The rest of you will have to introduce yourselves when we get back, it's getting late," Tor says as he inclines his head towards the door. The men start to mutter but they make their way towards the door, "We will have a party in your honour soon," Tor says as he walks past me, "Ulrich, let me know when Draco arrives."

"Will do," Ulrich replies, I realize that he has still got his arm around my shoulders, his height feeling protective, his warmth surrounding me. I don't know how long I will have with this man, but for now I will ride this dream and see where it will take me.

ULRICH 9

"Is this any welcome, where's the party?" Burkhart teases as he walks in with his mate at his side.

"Burkhart, you straggly ass," Colborn says from where he's standing by the bar, "thought you would never get here."

"Missed us, did you?" Brandr says as he also walks in, as soon as I see his mate Aria, I try to clear my mind. Anastasia went up to the room earlier on. But my mind is still filled with thoughts of her. I would rather keep my thoughts to myself instead of someone else knowing what I'm thinking. Walking towards them with a smile on my face, I see Bjarni and Draco walking in, their women walking ahead of them.

"Where is everyone?" Bjarni asks in a booming voice, I see his woman look over her shoulder and smile at him. Now when I look at these hardened men before me, I finally understand how they can be so powerful, so dangerous and yet be completely and absolutely dominated by these women that are their mates. Now that I am mated, I realize how absolutely consuming our bond is.

"They had to take care of some business; I'm sure Tor will tell you all about it once he gets back," I reply, which has Draco looking at me, his eyes not missing anything as he takes everything in.

"Ulrich," Burkhart calls, "hey my man, did I hear right?" he approaches me with a smile on his face.

"Depends what you are hearing," I state with a grin.

"Well, we were so shocked that we had to come here and see for ourselves, after all weren't you the one that said that you wouldn't be getting a mate," Burkhart says as he punches me on the arm, I notice that the women have walked towards one of the tables and are now sitting down while the men are starting to surround me which has my guard up.

"Yeah, looks like things change," Bjarni says as he comes to stand behind me

"I remember someone saying that having a mate was like cutting off your balls," Brandr says with a smirk as he looks at me knowing full well that I was the one that said that, but it was a joke.

"Tell me, Ulrich, do you feel less male?" Draco asks in a quiet tone as he stands right before me. To be honest, I feel anything but, my element has strengthened as I can feel its power since bonding with Anastasia also the feeling I get of overwhelming protectiveness towards my mate has me feeling all powerful knowing that I can protect her from most things.

"No, if anything, I feel more." Draco's eyes are intense as he looks at me.

"Is it true that you fought the bond?" Shit, how did he find out about that? Our mates are the most important thing to us, we are supposed to forget everything and everyone once we meet our mates. To be honest, ever since meeting Anastasia all I think about is her, so that much is true.

"Damn Draco, I wasn't expecting it to hit me like it did. One minute I was crawling out of bed from being with two women and the next I am hit sideways by all these feelings and fucking senses that I have never felt before."

"Fuck Draco, he sounds so despondent that I suddenly feel like weeping,," Burkhart quips and then I am being ambushed by Brandr, Burkhart as Bjarni holds me from behind.

"What the hell?" I grunt as they pick me up and start making their way outside.

"We got you a surprise," Draco says as we step outside and then I am being dropped on my feet again and they are stepping back with grins on their faces. I frown as I look at them and then around until my eyes land on my motorcycle.

"What the fuck?" I roar as I walk towards my bike. The letters that make up Anastasia's name are emblazed as if in flame and then ice on it. The artwork is amazing, and I know that Bjarni had a hand in it as he does amazing personalized artwork on bikes, but her name is all over my bike.

"How did you get my bike?" I ask.

"The guys brought it up when you were holed up in the room with your woman," Brandr says with a smirk, "Now your bike has been branded."

I look back at Bjarni seeing a grin on his face, "you know I respect your work, you are really talented but fuck did you have to put her name like that on my bike?" He just shrugs his grin widening, these fuckers are enjoying this.

"Don't worry brother, she will love it," Burkhart says with a straight face which has me wanting to punch him when I think of what Anastasia might think.

"Or think I'm a stalking freak," I mutter.

"Don't be so despondent I'm sure by now our women have found Anastasia and will welcome her into the MC," Draco says which has my stomach tightening, damn, Anastasia is already hard-headed. If they explain to her that as an Elemental my prime drive is to keep her happy she will definitely be impossible. I turn to make my way back inside; I need to find Anastasia before the women corrupt her completely, but before I make it inside Draco stops me by stepping before me.

"It will be okay, none of us would change a thing when it comes to our mates." I stand and stare at Draco, he isn't one to make unnecessary conversation. For him to be before me trying to appease my worries has me surprised. "Now let's go in, and don't worry the women won't corrupt her that much." At his statement I tense, did he read my mind? Can he read my mind? He turns and walks back inside without any indication, I turn back towards Bjarni that is right behind me.

"Can he read minds?" At my questions Bjarni just smiles and shrugs as he steps around me and makes his way inside.

"Come on, let's go have a drink to celebrate your bond," Burkhart says as he steps next to me and places his arm around my shoulders, guiding me inside. "I want to meet the poor woman that landed up with you," he quips

"Hey, I'm a pretty decent catch you know," I mutter as I

elbow him on his side jokingly.

"Yeah, like a worm," Brandr teases as he walks past, I notice that the women aren't in the bar area any longer which has my stomach knotting with nerves. I have heard all about how strong willed they can be, but I have also heard about how much they have helped the MC when it was time to bring down the Keres. I know that with time Anastasia will want to be with me, that she will understand, but the question is how long will it take her? After being with her, all I want to do is take her again, and again. When I was introducing her to the others, it was so good to see how well she joked with them even though I felt like taking her away from everyone and keeping her only to myself. I knew that doing that was important not only to her and our bond but to the brothers too.

We might not always see eye to eye, but we would die for each other and I need that when it comes to my mate. I want her to be protected and safe at all times even if I'm not around and I know that we might have our arguments, but every single one of the men will die before letting a woman come to harm especially one that belongs to another brother.

Asger hands me a beer as I take a seat at the bar turning my back to the counter I look at the others, Draco and his men might not be part of the Cape Town chapter but they are the founding chapter and as such we have the utmost respect for them as they have fought alongside all the chapters to keep the Elemental's safe when we still didn't have a cure for our rage. I close my eyes trying to sense Anastasia and sense her close, her energy is calm which tells me that if the other women found her, they are not upsetting her.

"I hear that you have some of the kidnappers in the basement," Draco states as he looks at Colborn that nods at him. "Have you been able to find anything else out?"

"No, they all have the same story that they collect the women from a specific location and take them to a house which they are responsible for. When they get a text message to take them somewhere else they drop them off and leave," Asger states as he comes to sit next to me.

"I think that they know more than they are saying, like who are they working for, how do they get paid," I mutter, I know that the gangs might not know much as they just pick the women up and deliver them to someone but the men that are actually keeping them before transporting them somewhere will know more I'm sure.

"I agree with you," Brandr says, "but we will find out soon enough if they know anything else." At his statement I frown, "If you guys don't mind, Burkhart and I will ask them some questions and I will have Aria help us to see if there are any other answers that they are not voicing." When I realize what they want to do I nod. Damn, who needs interrogations when you have someone like her around?

Maybe Draco can't read minds, or he would be the one interrogating the men, wouldn't he? I look over at Draco and see his lips kick up as he looks at me. Fuck, he can read minds.

"Well, it can't hurt, and whatever you find out will come in real handy. We thought that we would figure out who is shipping them, but what we found was a container that was registered under a fictitious name," I state

"Celmund has been combing through shipping companies but their systems aren't always the easiest to go through and most of them use paperwork as they haven't heard of technology," Bjarni says sarcastically, "we need someone that knows the shipping industry inside and out, like that they know what they are looking for and their way around their systems." I look towards the door sensing Anastasia and see her standing in the doorway a frown on her face, Katrina and Aria standing behind her.

"I do," she says as she takes a step forward. The men are all looking at her now. Katrina walks towards Draco and slides onto his lap and kisses him on the cheek, it is amazing to all of us how a man as powerful as Draco found a woman that can keep up with him, and not be intimidated by his power.

I stand and make my way towards my woman as Aria, Saskia and Gabriela also step around Anastasia and make their way towards their mates. "What do you mean Vixen?" she looks at me and frowns.

"My job, I work for a shipping company. Well, actually I practically ran the company as the owner gave me free rein," she states with a shrug. How did I not know this? I wanted to know about her gift, but I didn't make the time to find out about her life, I will rectify that at the earliest possible time.

"Well damn, we had a solution right here," Colborn says as he looks at me with a raised brow.

"Why do you need to know about shipping details?" she asks, looking at me.

"They were going to smuggle you across on a ship and the other women that they have kidnapped have all been taken on ships." At the mention of her abduction I see her flinch, which has my anger rising at the fuckers behind all of this.

"If I can get to my computer, then I can get most of the information that you need," she replies, taking her hand I turn fully towards the others.

"Do you need your computer, or can any computer do as long as you have your passwords?" Colborn asks

"There are some things that I might be able to check

online, but most of the ships have to log in with the port on what their cargo will be, usually we should be able to pick it up from there especially if we find a company or a person that sends items with different shipping companies or if the items are completely different from one container to another. We can also pick it up on who checks the container or if their container is one of those that never gets checked."

"We will get you a laptop, and then we will get you to talk to our tech guy Celmund that will help you get into anything you are finding difficult to get into," Draco states as he looks around Katrina's shoulder.

I don't want Anastasia to feel pressured into doing anything, I can feel the slight tremor in her hand and know that hacking into the shipping network isn't something she is feeling comfortable with. "Are you okay with that?" I ask.

"If it helps stop more women getting kidnapped and treated the way they treated me, then I'm more than willing to help." I can't stop myself from kissing her, lifting my hand I cradle her cheek as I lower my head and kiss her lips tenderly, feeling her tense. My woman isn't just fiery, but she's courageous too.

ANASTASIA 10

Meeting some of the men was nerve-racking, especially Tor as it was clear that he is a man that is used to leading and being obeyed. It is clear that he isn't someone not to be trifled with, all the men are dangerous, which it is clear to see, but I feel a sense of belonging here that I have never felt before. Being introduced by Ulrich to his brothers was clearly an honour, as it was evident from the way everyone treated me that Ulrich doesn't do this often.

I think back to when Ulrich touched me, every time he touches me it's like a spark is ignited. I don't know if what he says is true, but what I know is that he can make me forget everything with a stroke of a finger or a simple look. I came up earlier with the excuse that I needed to rest, but in truth I just needed some breathing space away from him to think.

There is a knock on the bedroom door which startles me, sitting up in bed I frown. Who could it possibly be? I swear if it's Camille I will just shut the door. Walking towards the door, I am surprised to see four women standing on the other side of the door. "Hi," one of them says as she steps forwards and hugs me.

"Oh, ignore Gabriela, she loves her hugs," one says as

she slips past us into the room.

"Hi," I reply, unsure what else to do when I'm ambushed by a group of women. I swear if they are more working girls here at the club coming to ask me questions about why I am now his old lady, I will kick them out.

"As Katrina said, I am Gabriela, Bjarni's mate and I am so pleased to meet another addition to our girl power." I don't know who Bjarni is, but from what she is saying she must be another of the old ladies.

"Let her breathe, you are overwhelming her, she doesn't even know what you are talking about." I turn my head and encounter a stunningly beautiful women with long dark brown hair. "Hi, I'm Saskia and I'm Burkhart's woman which you won't know who he is because we are from the Nurture Valley chapter." At her statement I realize who they must be.

"Is that Draco's men?" I ask.

"Yip, that's my man," Katrina says with a grin from where she's sitting on the bed, I look to my right and see the other woman standing there in the doorway, this one has straight black hair and stunning blue eyes, these four women are all stunning. I feel awkward standing between them with my curly hair and freckles.

"You are beautiful, I love your hair," she says with a gentle smile, "I am Aria and Brandr's other half."

"Nice to meet all of you." I still feel a little ambushed to be honest by they all seem so nice.

"We are here to welcome you to the Elemental's MC, as the women behind these yummy men," Gabriela says with a wink, "we are what drives them." With that she grins.

"Stop being a perv woman," Saskia quips as she elbows her, one thing she is right about these men are all yummy. I wonder if the ones in their chapter are just as delicious.

"They are even better, or I think so." My head snaps towards Aria, did I say that out loud? At my thought, she shakes her head. "No, you didn't." Oh hell no, she is listening to my thoughts.

"Stop doing that, you are going to freak her out before we can even talk to her," Katrina mutters

"Too late," I state staring at Aria.

"We all have gifts, each one in a different way. Aria just likes to show off," Saskia says as she pulls her tongue out at Aria playfully. That means that what Ulrich said about the women having gifts is true.

"I think it's time we explain to you about who the Elemental's are, what they are, and how we fit in," Aria says as she also makes her way towards the bed and takes a seat next to Katrina.

"Let's just say that they are not exactly human, but you have had sex with Ulrich, so you know that," Katrina says with a wink.

"They do excel at that, don't they?" Gabriela says with a smile.

"ANYWAY," Saskia says loudly to bring them back to the purpose of their visit, "As elemental's they can each bend a specific element, in Ulrich's case I think it's fire like Burkhart." At her statement I nod, I can feel my heart racing at the fact that what Ulrich tried to explain is true. "The elemental's only have one mate, when they find that mate everything changes for them. The only women that are mated to the elemental's are women with gifts like us."

"What's your gift?" Katrina asks, which has me tensing, "all I have to do is touch someone and I will know their truth," she states. Wow, so one can hear people's thoughts and the other one knows the truth about people just by touching them. I am very inadequate next to their gifts.

"I can make ice, nothing special." At my comment I see their eyes widen.

"You mean that you turn things into ice, same way as Ulrich turns things into fire?" Gabriela asks

"I guess," I mutter, not yet sure what Ulrich can do with the fire he manifested.

"That is so great, it means that you can cool down a person when they have a fever or cool down a fiery situation. And after meeting Ulrich a couple of times and being here at the club with the bunch of men a few times, I am sure you will have many opportunities to do that." I had never thought about it that way but I guess that I can do that, I know that sometimes when my parents were fighting I would wish for them to calm down and they would, but I never once thought that I was the one doing that by cooling their rage.

"Do you have to touch someone, or can you project cold towards them?" Saskia asks as she too goes and sits on the other side of Katrina.

"I have never tried to project it; in truth I have always tried not to use my gift." At my words Gabriela throws up her hands.

"It's so sad that we all had to do that before meeting our men, but you will be happy to know that you can use your gift as much as you want now and you will find that it's not just Ulrich that gets stronger but your gift grows too with time."

"When you say they're not quite human, are they aliens?" Katrina claps her hands with a laugh

"Yip, I sure think Draco is a bit of an alien sometimes," she quips.

"Ignore her," Saskia says with a laugh, "they have been

on earth for centuries, they are more from earth then most humans are. Has Ulrich told you how old he is?" I tense, what does she mean?

"No, why?" I see them looking at each other before Saskia answers.

"They have been living for a very long time, and now you will be too."

"What does that mean?" I ask, wanting to know exactly what they are trying to imply.

"Well you know the dinosaurs; I think Draco was one of them," Katrina says with a straight face before Aria elbows her on the side which has them all laughing.

"If he hears you say that you will be in trouble," Gabriela says with a wink.

"Damn, I must remember to say it in front of him," she quips.

"You are such a hussy," Gabriela quips with a laugh.

"Well aren't you one to talk?" They all laugh which makes me smile, I have never been around a group of women like this four before. "But we are deviating, Anastasia here wants to know what we mean."

"On the way here, I asked Brandr how old Ulrich was and he says that his definitely in his three hundred's." At her statement I laugh, now I know they are pulling my leg.

"Okay, you had me there for a while," I say as I shake my head, I wonder who put them up to it.

"We aren't joking, they really are old, and we luckily inherit that from them." I know my mouth is gaping open, but I seem to not be able to close it. Are they for real?

"You seem a little pale, maybe you should sit down after everything you have just gone through," Gabriela says as she walks up to me and places her arm around my shoulders, guiding me to the bed.

"Now don't joke, please tell me the truth."

"That is the truth sweetheart, you are bonded to an Elemental and your life expectancy has just increased. You will find that you don't really get sick like you used to, you will feel stronger," Aria says as I sit on the bed, my back against the headboard which has the three of them turning so that they can see me. Gabriela walks around the bed and takes a seat on the other side. My head is spinning with all the information that they are giving me and I'm still not sure if I can believe them or not, but I guess time will tell.

"There are a few things you need to know," Saskia says, "Elemental's are possessive, they do not like other men near their woman. Once you bonded you will find that you cannot be long without your mate, without physically missing him."

"There is constant danger, even though now it has calmed since we found a cure for their fury," Gabriela says.

"What do you mean?" I ask with a frown.

"Because Elemental's live so long, if they don't find their mate then fury overwhelms them, and they would become Keres which is a similar version of the Elemental's but evil. Fortunately, a few years back we found a cure which calms their rage, and which stops them from turning into Keres," Aria explains.

"Yes, things have calmed down considerably since then, but in Cape town there are still some Keres that have been difficult to find and the men think that they are the ones behind the kidnapping of all these women," Katrina states, "Draco was telling me that the Keres have involved gangs and that makes the situation unstable." Yes, I remember the two men that took me initially, they looked like they might belong to a gang with their tattoos and the way they were dressed.

"All you need to know is that now you are a part of the Elemental's MC, the men will die before they let anyone hurt you and we are but a phone call away if you ever need a woman to talk to."

"But I have a life, I don't even live in Cape Town, how can I possibly just give everything up and join a motorcycle club?" even just saying the words it sounds crazy.

"You know that this is so much more than just a motorcycle club, with time you will see that there is no other place that you would rather be than right by your man, and the men here at the club will become like family." This can't be true; did I knock my head or am I still in captivity and hallucinating all of this?

"No sweetheart, it is all quite true," Aria answers my thoughts.

"Now enough talk, shall we go down and introduce you to our men?" Katrina says, which has me hesitant as I'm not sure if I want to ever leave this room again.

"Before we go down, you are now the first mate in the Cape Town Chapter. You will be the one that welcomes the other women when they bond with one of the men here, and you will have to be the one that explains all of this to them," Gabriela says, "Jas was the first one in Nurture Valley, she would have come with us but twisted her ankle when she crashed her motorcycle. Since then that Wulf has her on lockdown," at that the women laugh.

"That wasn't a crash, she forgot to put her feet down when she stopped the bike, you can hardly call that a crash when the bike had stopped." At Katrina's statement the others grin which has me once again smiling at their camaraderie.

"When will another of the men bond?" I'm not sure I am prepared to welcome anyone into a world which I am not sure about yet.

"Don't worry, it can be months, years or even centuries," Aria says as she pats my leg before standing. "Now come, no use hiding in here. Let's go down and see what they are all up to."

We make our way towards the bar; the women walking behind me as I guide the way. As I enter the bar I hear the men talking. "Celmund has been combing through shipping companies but their systems aren't always the easiest to go through and most of them use paperwork as they haven't heard of technology." The man talking is a bear of a man, his voice gruff and I can hear the irritation in it which I completely agree with from what he says, one of my pet peeves working for the shipping industry was always the way documents were filled, "we need someone that knows the shipping industry inside and out, like that they know what they are looking for and their way around their systems."

"I do," I say before I realize what I am doing, I can feel everyone's eyes on me now which is a little unnerving, but I was just surrounded by men earlier and survived, I'm sure I will now too. I sought out Ulrich, only to see him approaching me, which has me relaxing a little knowing that he is close.

"What do you mean Vixen?" What does he mean,

doesn't he know that I work for a shipping company?

"My job, I work for a shipping company. Well, actually I practically ran the company as the owner gave me free rein."

"Well damn, we had a solution right here," Colborn says which has my curiosity rising at what he means.

"Why do you need to know about shipping details?" I ask looking at Ulrich.

"They were going to smuggle you across on a ship and the other women that they have kidnapped have all been taken on ships." At the reminder of what I have just gone through I tense, if women are being smuggled in ships and I can do something about it then I will definitely help.

"If I can get to my computer, then I can get most of the information that you need," I reply, Ulrich takes my hand and I feel friction run up my arm.

"Do you need your computer, or can any computer do as long as you have your passwords?" Colborn asks

"There are some things that I might be able to check online, but most of the ships have to log in with the port on what their cargo will be, usually we should be able to pick it up from there especially if we find a company or a person that sends items with different shipping companies or if the items are completely different from one container to another. We can also pick it up on who checks the container or if their container is one of those that never gets checked."

"We will get you a laptop, and then we will get you to talk to our tech guy Celmund that will help you get into anything you are finding difficult to get into." I'm guessing the man talking is Draco as Katrina is all over his lap, and Damn she wasn't joking when she said the men were hot. When he smiles, I'm sure those dimples would stop traffic?

"Are you okay with that?" Ulrich asks which has me looking at him, I was so distracted by Draco's smile that I completely got side-tracked from the subject.

"If it helps stop more women getting kidnapped and treated the way they treated me, then I'm more than willing to help." I see Ulrich's eyes darken and a tender smile appear on his face just as he places his hand on the side of my face and gives me a tender kiss in front of everyone.

"Maybe you should go back to your room and take Ulrich with you," Katrina quips as Ulrich lifts his head grinning.

"I want to introduce you to some of the men from our mother chapter, and to our president Draco." At his statement I look over to the men, they all nod in greeting and then my eyes clash with Draco's and I tense.

"Welcome Anastasia, you have now joined our most prized gifts, our women." At his words, I feel a shiver rush down my spine.

ULRICH 11

After introducing Anastasia, Colborn went upstairs to get his laptop. Burkhart phoned Celmund that was more than happy to setup anything that my woman might need. "I should phone my boss; he might be able to help." At her comment I tense, I don't want anyone alerted about what we are looking for before we actually have any information. I place my hand over Anastasia's that is laying next to the laptop and squeeze gently.

"Maybe we hold off talking to anyone until we know what we are dealing with." At my statement she turns her head to look at me, a frown on her face.

"Are you telling me not to speak to my boss?" there is a tone of irritation in her voice.

"We don't know anything about him, as far as we know he might be involved." At my reply, her frown turns into a glare.

"I have been working for Mr. Smith for years and I can tell you that he wouldn't be involved in something like this." At the defence of this man I tense, why the hell is she so defensive of a man that is her boss?

"Why are you so defensive of this man?" my voice is low as I lean towards her, I see her tense and her eyes sharpen in anger.

"Are you insinuating that I have something going on with my boss?" I hadn't thought about that but now at the thought of another man touching my woman my whole-body tenses as my vision starts to sharpen. If that son of a bitch ever touched my women, he is dead.

"Do you?" At my question I suddenly yelp as my hand feels like it has been scorched by flame, but fire will never burn me, pulling my hand back I feel its coldness through my bones. "Did you just freeze my hand?"

"You're an ass." With those words, she suddenly stands and turns making her way out of the bar area.

"Not so fast," I mutter as I take off after her, grabbing

her arm I turn her around and push her against the wall near the door. "Don't even think of freezing me again because I will use my fire to thaw you."

"Let go of me, you think that I have something going with my boss?"

"Why are you so defensive of him?" I ask instead of answering her question, which has her pushing at my chest, when I don't budge, she slaps my chest angrily grunting in anger.

"He's old enough to be my father, I wouldn't sleep with someone at work." At her reply I relax knowing that she's not defending the man because of any hidden feelings.

"Then why do you defend him?"

"He's my boss, half of the time he doesn't' even know what is going on in the company if it wasn't for me." At her statement I nod and then I start to lower my head to kiss her as my body is well aware of her nearness and is responding, but she shoves at me glaring.

"Don't you dare kiss me when you have just accused me of having a thing going with my boss." She will learn that in our relationship I'm the one that wears the pants and not the other way around. Letting go of her one arm my hand rises to her neck and then I am pulling her closer into my arms, I hear the air woosh out of her lungs as she is crushed against me before I take her lips in a possessive kiss that will show her that she is mine. I start feeling the coldness penetrating my skin and know that she is fighting this with her gift. Well, two can play this game. I bring my body heat up knowing that she will feel the heat seeping into her body, melting her frost.

This woman is like a hurricane, she has blown all past beliefs of being single right out of my mind when I met her but what has completely and utterly caught my attention is her fire. Anastasia may be Ice, but she has a fire burning in her soul that will rival my very own. She makes me burn with a passion that will ignite and erupt like it never has before.

"Will the two of you fucking stop that," Dag mutters. "I've already had a shower today." The men arrived earlier on today, Tor and Draco disappeared a couple of minutes later as the women except for Aria were shown to where they will be sleeping. Brandr, Burkhart and Aria have gone down to interrogate the men that we have caught. Dag, Asger and Colburn were sitting near the bar talking and Bjarni was sitting across from us before we started arguing.

Pulling back, I am surprised to see the floor wet and there is moisture in the air looking a lot like fog. I hear Anastasia's surprised intake of breath as she looks around. "Did we do this?" she asks.

"Yeah, at least if we ever have to hide, we know what to

do," Colburn states as he looks at us.

"What the hell happened here?" Tor asks as he walks in, Draco a step behind him.

"Fire and Ice seem to give us fog when in disagreement," Asger states with a straight face.

"Just think, you would make a fortune in a country that has draught," Colburn mutters as he takes a sip of his beer, which has me lifting my finger at him.

"Looks like you have one weapon that you didn't have before," Draco states with a wink at Tor.

"Yeah, we might just need trackers to find each other though," Tor mutters as he glares at me.

"I think you will look quite good with one of those miners lights Tor," Bjarni teases as he grins at him, "it will light up those golden locks of yours, the women won't be able to resist you then." Tor looks at him, his lips rising in amusement at his quip.

"Who said they can resist me now?" Tor states as he raises his brow, before Bjarni can reply Burkhart walks in, he looks up and around seeing the moisture in the air and then shrugs before he looks at us.

"Does anyone know what DUB36N28EI means, one of the fuckers downstairs apparently was projecting that the whole time that we have been questioning them. Aria thought that it might be something important."

"Sounds like coordinates to me," Dag says as he scratches his chin.

"DUB could stand for Durban, but because there is an I at the end it means it is international coordinates, therefore DUB stands for Dubai, and yes the thirty six N stands for thirty six North and twenty eight East," Anastasia says as she looks at Burkhart.

"Are you saying it's a shipping reference?" Tor asks with a frown.

"It sounds like a shipping reference," she says as she steps around me towards the laptop, "I will look into that reference and see what ship it is and if it has already left port." She sits back down before the laptop and starts to type. After a couple of minutes, she looks over her shoulder at Burkhart, "It says here that, that ship left port three days ago."

"That must have been the ship that they were going to take Anastasia in," I state as in come to stand behind her.

"Damn, would be nice if we caught a break," Dag mutters, "now we will have to start from scratch again and try and find another ship that they will be using."

"At least we know that they were transporting them to Dubai, maybe the others have been taken there too," Colburn says, "maybe we can get someone on to that side to look at things."

"Actually, we might be able to find something," Anastasia says as she looks around at the men, "If they have always transported the women to the same place then I can call up how many times this reference has been used in the last year, and then we can look at which companies are sending there and how often." I can see her frown as she thinks of all the steps, she can use to track down these fuckers.

"It might be a long list, wont it as I assume there are quite a few things being transported to Dubai," Burkhart asks

"Yes, the list might be long, but I can then reduce it by who the official is that opens these containers. If we find a set of containers from the same company being opened by the same official, then we know that there is something fishy happening."

"Can you do that from here, or do you need anything else to get that information?" Tor asks as he approached us.

"For the main list I will be able to get it from here, but when it comes to who the official is, then I need to get into international database and I don't have the access here as that was all on my laptop," Anastasia says which has me placing my hand on her shoulder and squeezing gently to try calm her worries.

"Celmund will help you get into the database, when you are ready let Ulrich know and he will contact Celmund."

I nod to Draco; I prefer this option than to let Anastasia go all the way back to work. I know that sooner or later she will want to see her parents and she will want to inform her boss that she is fine but first I would rather first find out if anyone she knows was involved in her kidnapping.

"Who knew about your gift besides your parents?" She tenses under my hand.

"What?" she asks, lifting her head back to look at me.

"They are kidnapping mostly women with gifts like yours, someone must have known about your gift for them to find out." At my statement, she scowls and then shakes her head.

"Only my parents knew about what I can do, and the doctors." At her reply, Bjarni sits forward.

"Who were the doctors?" Bjarni asks, "we have found with other women that they are getting the information from clinics which the women have frequented." He looks back at Draco, "we thought we had got all the lists, looks like they might have more."

"It can't be, I was just a kid when I had tests done." Then she raises her hand to touch mine as she half turns on the chair to look at me, "but they did contact me about a year ago, they said that they had a little girl that had the same symptoms as me and if I would be willing to go in and do some more tests so that they can compare to hers and try and find a cure."

"The fuckers most probably wanted to kidnap you then already," Dag says.

"You don't think that they really had a little girl, did they?" I can hear the worry in her voice as she looks at me, placing a hand on her cheek I lean down kissing her lips gently.

"No vixen, they didn't have another girl there. More than likely they just wanted to get you there," I state as I stand up straight again.

"Why didn't you go?" Colburn asks as he comes to sit next to Bjarni.

"I thought that if the girl was like me, then she would realize that it isn't an illness, I had so many needles and tests done when I was there that I am reluctant to go anywhere near a needle again," She murmurs.

"Good thing you mated to an Elemental then, we don't get sick," Burkhart says as he turns to go back downstairs.

"I'll come with you," Tor says looking back at Draco that nods. The three of them make their way out. With Aria getting the information from their minds, we might find out more than we have in a couple of months. Just then Dane walks in from outside a scowl on his face as he looks around.

"What's up?" Dag asks as Dane starts making his way towards where the others disappeared. He stops then lifts his phone in frustration.

"Suraya found her mate," Dane grunts which has me tensing, fuck, Tor is going to be in a mood. Suraya is one of the women that Draco and his men found, at the time Saskia, Burkhart's mate and another four women were being hunted by the Keres when they found them. Draco asked that we come down and collect the women and transport them to their families. Right from the beginning Tor and Suraya had a hate, love relationship going. Suraya has the gift of attraction and Tor was attracted; he tries to keep away from her as much as he can, but we all know that she is out of bounds.

"Good thing it's you telling him," Dag states as he winks at a disgruntled Dane.

"Who is she mated to?" I ask curious to know why she hasn't found her mate until now, most of the women that we have found if they have a mate that mate is identified at the time.

"It was one of the Keres, apparently he was cured and is back to being an Elemental and now going to be mated," Dane updates as he shrugs.

"You want to go for a ride?" I ask leaning down close to Anastasia's ear, I see the skin on her arms rise in goosebumps as my nearness which makes me smile.

"Now?" she asks breathlessly.

"Yeah, I don't want to be here when Tor hears the news," I mutter, to be honest I don't think Tor will be that upset, but he does dislike losing and this he will see as losing one of his women to someone else.

"Okay, but I must warn you I have never been on a motorcycle before." At her words I smile, she doesn't know what she has been missing she will see what it feels like when flying. To have my woman all to myself, close behind me has my body reacting at the thought. When before all I wanted was to ride my bike solo now, I can't think of anything better than having my mate with me.

ANASTASIA 12

When we got back from our ride most of the men were in the bar area, Aria and Katrina were also there sitting at one of the tables talking. I also saw Camille, Tanya, Monica, and Andy sitting with some of the men, from what Katrina informed me later these women are the clubs blossoms, or that is what the men call the women.

I suspected about their functions at the club, but for it to be confirmed that these women are here for any of the men's pleasures has my anger rising. Ulrich hasn't shown any signs of closeness with any of the women, but just the fact that they are here for his pleasure if he ever wants it has my very skin crawling with rage. That is until Aria appeases some of the rage with the fact that once an Elemental is mated, he doesn't want any other women again. From what she says they feel repulsed by the touch of another woman.

I had a really nice ride with Ulrich, that is, once he slowed down. The man is a lunatic on a bike, but it is so exhilarating riding through the streets at night with no one but the wind, the motorcycle and the man before you. The camaraderie that built when we were out riding starts to crash the longer I sit in the bar area hearing the blossoms laughing and simpering over the men. Ulrich is sitting at the bar talking to Garth. Every now and again our eyes clash and he winks or smiles at me and in those moments everything seems fine but then I look to the side and encounter the women and everything comes flooding back again.

Katrina has just got up to go to the bathroom when Aria leans towards me complaining about how hungry she is which has both of us walking towards the kitchen to go and raid what is there. We are laughing at a story she is telling me about one of the other women in their chapter, Nova, and what a real terror she is when Tanya and Monica walk in. Looking over my shoulder to see who has entered I grunt. Great, I leave the bar and here they are after us.

"Is it true that you are Ulrich's old lady?"

"Tanya!" Monica says in an exasperated tone

"It seems like it," I mutter closing the fridge, all humour

leaving me.

"I wonder why he would choose someone like you to be his old lady, you will never make him happy you know that don't you?" I hear Aria gasping from besides me and Monica's perplexed expression as she takes a step away from Tanya.

"What would you know about it, from what I hear you aren't an old lady." I face her fully, taking a step towards her.

"I know Ulrich better than you do," Tanya says as she gives me a false smile.

"It's okay, I wasn't planning on knowing him when I first met him, but I will make sure to get to know him as we continue." I look towards Aria and incline my head towards the door, "shall we get back?" I ask and receive Aria's curt nod.

"You see, I told you she doesn't have the fire that he is used to in bed," Tanya comments to Monica

"Enough Tanya, are you crazy?" Monica says as she turns to make her way out of the kitchen. My temper snaps, how dare she judge me and try to place a rift between Ulrich and me.

"What would you know about how I am in bed or not? You know nothing about me." I can feel the anger racing through my body at her audacity and at what she is implying.

"I know that you won't be able to satisfy him, just a couple of days ago he had Monica and me. How would a stuck-up bitch like you know how to satisfy a man like him?" Hearing her tell me that which I was most dreading has my blood running cold, I knew that I shouldn't have had any hopes where he is concerned, it is clear as day that he is an unruly rebel, not conforming to what is expected of people. How could I believe that he would actually want to be with me, the naughtiest thing I ever done was go skinny dipping with one of my friends when I was a teenager and that's because we knew for a fact that no one would be coming home and that no one would be able to see us in the darkness as her house had huge walls that kept out any prying eyes.

"Doesn't look like you satisfied him at all, or he wouldn't have come to find me, now would he?" And with those words I don't stay to hear anymore snide remarks, instead I make my way out of the kitchen and towards the stairs. The last person I want to see right now is Ulrich, If I see him now, I will freeze his balls for being such a man whore.

"Anastasia," I hear Aria call but I am too furious to talk right now, "don't listen to what she was saying, she's just a mean, ungrateful cow that will get what she has coming to her." I don't stop but continue my way.

"What's going on?" I hear Katrina say as she walks out

of the bathroom as I walk past without stopping. I hear Aria explaining to her, but I don't stop. I walk up the stairs and into the bedroom, locking the door behind me.

"Aargh," I mutter angrily as I start pacing from one side of the room to the other, I am so angry that I could just scream. I feel the coldness seeping from me, but instead of stopping it like I usually do, I welcome the cold as I let it spread around the room. I should have frozen her tongue, because all I can imagine now is Ulrich in bed with those two women and its driving me crazy. There is a knock on the door, but I don't pay it any attention.

I just want to be alone for now with my thoughts, I feel a hurt so deep that I have never felt before not even when my first boyfriend called me ice queen because I couldn't give him the attention that he wanted. I know that what she said happened before Ulrich met me but the fact that two women that he slept with, had sex with who knows how many times are here in this house right under our noses and every time he looks at them he will remember. The thought of him with those two women is filling me with so much fury that I can't even cry.

I don't care that it was before we met; I don't care that he didn't know me yet. If he only has one mate, then why would he be such a whore and sleep with two women at the same time. Aria says that Elemental's don't have the same pleasure with other women like they have with their mates, well I wonder what she will think now when she knows that he didn't just enjoy one woman but two at the same time.

He didn't like it so much that he had to double the experience; I think sarcastically. I don't know how long I am pacing this room when there is a bang on the door and then I hear Ulrich swear. "What the fuck Anastasia?" he roars. Only now when I look, do I see that the door is frozen solid. There is a thick slab of ice around the door and some on the floor and walls. I look around in surprise at how much ice there is, I have never done this before and in such a short amount of time. Well, let him try get through that door now.

I turn towards the bed to go and sit down but I notice that there is a layer of ice on the top of the bed too. Damn, not that handy when I don't have anywhere to sit down. "What the hell did you think you were doing?" he asks angrily from the other side of the door.

"Go away," I mutter, too angry with him to speak.

"No, and you can't do this every time you get into a tizzy." At his words my anger rises again, how dare he tell me what I can and cannot do.

"Go away, I don't want to speak to you," I state as I walk towards the door

"They told me you are upset," he states which has me gasping, "I don't see why you're angry." I know I am standing here with my mouth open in disbelief, how dare he make it sound like I'm being petty and picking on something being childish. I don't know if I can do this but I sure will try, closing my eyes I think of him and think of his tongue getting cold, if he doesn't leave then I will make him shut up.

"Fuck, what do you. . ." he mutters, I can hear his voice is gravely, and it sounds like he has something in his mouth. "Get away from the fucking door because this door is coming down," he suddenly roars. I have hardly stepped to the side frowning, doubtful, there is no way he can break down the door as it is frozen solid when I hear a crack and then the door is being thrown back against the bed.

"Are you mad?" I ask in surprise, looking at the hinges hanging from the doorframe, "You could have killed me if I was still standing behind that door." He is glaring at me as he steps through the door and then his foot slides from under him on the ice and he is roaring as he loses his footing and crashes to the ground.

All I can do is stare at him as he lays on the floor stunned, and then he turns his head, glaring at me. Suddenly the ice all around him is melting and I can feel heat rising from the floor. He stands, his eyes not leaving me not even for a second. "Don't ever try to keep me away from you, because nothing, not even you will keep me from you." He starts walking towards me, and even though I try to hold my place, the anger in his eyes has me stepping back.

"You are mine; you do not block me from you." His voice is low in anger, "and if you ever try to freeze me again, I will spank you." At his words I gasp in surprise.

"I'm not yours, and you wouldn't dare." Before I can even blink, I find myself being lifted off the floor and then he is placing me face down over his lap as he sits on the now wet bed. "Ulrich, don't you . . ." before I can finish my sentence, he is bringing down his palm flat on my ass.

"Aargh," I screech but he doesn't listen or pay any attention as I try to wiggle off his lap, instead his hand comes down again stinging my ass cheek. "Oh, you caveman," I scream as he spanks me again, after another couple of spanks I stop fighting as my ass is now feeling like it's on fire.

He spanks me two more times before he finally pulls me up to my feet; I look up at him and glare. I can sense the anger still coursing through his body, his every muscle is tense, and his eyes are hard with his ire. His head turns and then he is looking around the room which has me following his gaze, to my dismay I see most of the things are wet, the door is laying half on the bed the other half on the floor. I see Haldor and Eirik standing outside the door, a look of surprise on their faces as they look at both of us.

Suddenly Ulrich is turning and walking out of the room,

his shoulders tense as he leaves. I start to follow, I'm about to argue when Eirik steps inside, "Let him be sugar, give him a minute." At his words, I tense.

"This isn't all my fault, you know," I mutter as I look around again, "do you know that he slept with Tanya and Monica at the same time." I know that I am sounding prudish, but that man is unbelievable.

"It was before you sweetheart, trust me when I tell you that he wants nothing to do with any other women except you." Haldor states as he walks towards the door and picks it up, these doors are solid wood but the way he is handling it, it would make anyone think that it weights nothing.

"How am I supposed to believe that when every time I look around, they are there, and she definitely won't keep away from him the way she spoke." My anger is rising again when I think of Tanya, "I do not share, and I will not be in a relationship where I'm not sure about my man." I suddenly tense when I realize what I just said. When did I start thinking of Ulrich as my man? And when did I start thinking of us as a relationship?

It is madness being in a relationship with a man like Ulrich; I feel my stomach knotting as I think of leaving and not being with Ulrich. My heart starts to race as I think of Ulrich coming up here and telling me that this won't work, that we are way too volcanic for it to work. I jump in surprise when Eirik comes to stand right before me.

"It will be fine, just let him cool down and then you two can figure out how not to destroy the rest of the club," Haldor says as he runs his fingers down the wall which is wet through. "Good thing Tor went out and might not notice when he comes back because he will be pissed to see this."

"I'm sorry." Now that I look around, I feel absolutely terrible at the destruction in the wake of Ulrich and my anger. The ground where Ulrich slipped is burned as if there was a great fire, I can just imagine at the heat that he was radiating to do that to the floor, good thing there is no carpet in here or it would have gone up in flames and then we would have burnt down the club.

"Its fine sugar, just keep away from my room okay," Eirik teases as he pulls the bedding off the bed. "Looks like you guys won't be able to sleep in here for a while, the mattress is wet through. I see Eirik pressing down with his palm and hear a sloshing sound.

"That water will never dry in there," I mutter, already thinking of buying a new mattress to pay Ulrich back for destroying his bed but then I gasp as I see Eirik lifting his hand and water lifting from the mattress up as if a reversed waterfall and through the air in particles into the bathroom. No way, I bring up my hands and rub at my eyes, but when I open them again, he is still pulling the water from the mattress and somehow driving it through the air into the bathroom.

"I'm guessing you are water element."Eirik looks over at me and smiles.

"What gave me away?" he quips just as Aria walks into the room followed by Saskia.

"Oh man, this place is trashed," Saskia says making me feel worse, I see Aria elbow Saskia and then she is walking up to me and hugging me, something that I never did much of before but which I find I like.

"Come Anastasia, let's go find you somewhere else to spend the night," Aria says as she draws her arm through mine and starts to guide me out of the room.

"Hey sugar, just try not to destroy something else tonight, okay." Eirik says.

"Don't be mean Eirik," Saskia says as we walk out of the room and I hear Eirik mutter.

"What did I say?"

ULRICH 13

As soon as I saw Aria and Katrina walking into the bar without Anastasia, I knew something was wrong. When they told me that Anastasia went rushing upstairs, I went after her only to find the door frozen solid. Fuck, she can freeze things like the ice pole. I was so damn furious that she would try to keep me away from her that I wasn't thinking straight when I threw her over my knee and spanked her.

I still don't know what the fuck has her in a rage, Aria and Katrina told me she was angry, but they didn't tell me why, I will find out what happened though. Rushing into the bar I look around and see Katrina sitting to the one side with Draco, Bjarni and Gabriela. "Why is she in a fucking mood?" I ask as I come to a stop in front of the table.

I see Draco turn his head towards me and by the look in his eye I know that I better be careful how I talk to his mate, but fuck Anastasia drives me out of her mind. "Did you ask her?" Katrina asks with a raised brow.

"She froze the room, I had to break the door to get in." Gabriela covers her mouth in surprise, Katrina claps as if it's the best thing she heard.

"Wow, that girl has the best gift," Katrina states as she places her hand over Draco's, "If you want to know why your girl was upset, you should go ask your two play friends over there." At her words I frown looking over my shoulder at who she's talking about. I see Dag and Colburn at the bar and there is Tanya and Monica sitting with Dane and Garth.

"Who?" I ask, looking back at her.

"You don't remember, your night of torrent play?" Katrina asks sarcastically, "Your little girlfriends don't have the same problem, they were very colourful in explaining to your mate about your games." Hearing the reason for Anastasia's anger I feel my body tensing. They told her that I was with both of them, shit. I snap around and see the women looking at me with guilty looks on their faces.

Striding towards them I feel the anger pumping through my veins. They know better than to mess with a brother's old lady. Dane looks up at me with a smile on his face, but the smile quickly tenses when he senses my anger. "Hey brother," he calls but I ignore him as I look directly at the women, I see Monica looking down at the table, but Tanya is looking directly at me, her posture confrontational.

"Did you two talk to my old lady?" I can hear the anger vibrating in my voice but if what Katrina said is true, then these two just jeopardized my bond and I won't let anyone ever come between my mate and me. They hurt Anastasia with their purposeful innuendos, I will not let anyone hurt my mate no matter what.

"It wasn't me," Monica states quietly, her eyes still down.

"She needed to hear the truth; she needs to know that if she wants to please you, she will have to get that stick out of her ass." I lose complete control at her mean words, one minute I am standing before them the next I am about to place my hands around her neck when I feel the weight barrelling into me.

"Calm down brother," I hear Colburn say but the thought that his women purposefully baited Anastasia, hurting her feelings, placing a wedge between us all because of her dislike for the mate has my reason leaving me as I push at Colburn's shoulders. Then there are arms holding me down from above and I see Dane hovering over me.

"Don't make me knock you out because of that bitch brother, we will deal with her calm down," Dane mutters. I can hear the women talking and someone shouting but I can't tell who it is as I try to calm the raging fury that is racing through my body.

"Get them out of here," I hear someone say.

"But I didn't do anything," I hear Monica cry out.

"Let me go," I mutter as I try to shrug both of them off me, finding a semblance of control but they aren't budging as they hold me down.

"What the fuck is going on here?" I hear Tor roar as he walks in.

"Looks like the blossoms were messing with Ulrich's old lady," Garth replies.

"Let him go," Tor orders.

"Stay calm, or I will knock your ass out," Dane mutters, his muscles vibrating as he pulls his hands away. Colburn looks at me intensely before he gets up from where he was straddling me and then stretches out his hand to help me up. Taking his hand, I stand and then turn to face Tor that is standing by the entrance door to the bar with his hands low on his hips.

"What happened?" He asks with a raised brow.

"Looks like Tanya decided that my woman isn't good

enough for me and needed to know about my earlier sexual encounters." At the words, I feel my stomach knot when I think about what Anastasia must have thought.

"She will be gone," Tor states as he starts to turn to walk out again but I stop him with my next words.

"Monica too." Instead of answering, he simply nods and then he is leaving.

"At least we still have Andy and Camille," Colburn quips as he wiggles his eyebrows.

"For now," Katrina says from where she's sitting, looking over my shoulder at he,r I see her smiling at me sweetly. "Mates don't like the idea of their men being around women they have slept with," she states with a shrug as she looks at Draco. "Just think how you would feel if it was reversed." At her words I tense, the thought of Anastasia sleeping with anyone has me wanting to kill someone. I see Draco scowling at her just before he places his hand behind her neck and pulls her towards him as he kisses her passionately.

"Oh no man," Garth mutters as he glares at me, "does that mean we have to get rid of the other two?"

"Maybe we can get some new blossoms in, ones that Ulrich didn't touch," Colburn states as he scratches his jaw and then grins, "Isn't a bad idea, maybe we just send Camille and Andy to one of our other chapters and get ourselves new help." The women at the club are the ones that usually cook our meals and do what is needed to maintain the place, not that they do a great job, but it's better than what we would do. If they are all gone, we will need to find more help. I should have found out why Anastasia was upset before going up to talk to her but where she is concerned all logic leaves me. I ignore the comments as I make my way towards my room only to stop outside when I see it empty. The door has been placed on the outside against the wall and the room has been cleaned. I will have to thank Eirik and Haldor for cleaning up but for now I must find Anastasia.

I close my eyes to sense her, but then snap them open again and look behind me to see Tor walking towards me. "What the hell happened here?" he grunts as he looks inside, good thing it's already cleaned or he wouldn't have been so calm.

"I had to break it down to get to Anastasia," I mutter, he raises a brow as he looks at me.

"Not going well, is it?" he asks

"She tried to freeze me." At my statement he grins.

"Looks like you found your match brother," he says as he slaps me on the back and then walks away. I grunt in reply as I once again close my eyes, trying to find the mate's essence. As an elemental our essence is bound together the moment, we mated therefore I will be able to find her anywhere as long as I'm close enough to feel her energy.

Turning to my left I make my way down the corridor and then turn left, I hear Anastasia talking before I draw closer, her voice is low, but I can hear everything she is saying. Being an elemental doesn't only come with a long life, but we can hear, smell, and see way better than a human can. Our strength and speed are also more advanced than humans.

You say we are destined to be together but look at the way we fight, how can I be with someone when all we do is fight. I tense when I hear Anastasia's doubts; I know that it is difficult for someone that is an elemental to understand the rightness of a bonded relationship but she should be able to feel the connection between us? Yes, we fight, but that is just because we are both hard-headed and want to be right. I won't let her think that we are not good together, she will realize how good we are together, I just need to show her.

I sense Aria and Saskia inside; I don't want to interrupt them when they are clearly trying to calm Anastasia. They will help her understand our bond, the elemental's drive and commitment to their mates. And when I join her, I will start by showing her how much I appreciate her. I have always been a success with the women, I won't start being a disappointment now with my very own mate.

Turning I make my way back downstairs, I will have to

ask someone to help and the only one that I know that can sweet talk like the devil himself is Colburn, he will teach me what to say and how to romance her. I'm used to women like the blossoms, women that will do anything to please us. To now encounter a woman that actually says no, a woman that is stubborn, that knows her own mind.

"You back?" Garth asks with a raised brow when I walk back into the bar.

"Yeah, I need to discuss something with Colburn." Colburn that is sitting next to him raises a brow. "Let's go for a walk," I mutter which has both men look at me in surprise, but Colburn nods and stands following me outside.

Looking around, I notice two of the prospects by the bikes having a smoke, I make my way towards the wall that surrounds the property and the club.

"I didn't know you wanted to go for a walk." Colburn quips, I don't reply and carry on walking as I try to think of a way of bringing up a way of what I need from him. "Come on Bro, just spit it out," he suddenly mutters stopping in his tracks.

"I need your help," I say as I also stop and look at him.

"Sure, what do you need?" he asks with a frown.

"I'm not a fucking poet, or one of those sensitive guys,"

I state and see him frown, "therefore I need you to teach me."

"What?" Colburn asks with a surprised look on his face, "are you saying that I'm a sensitive guy?"

"You are more sensitive to all these fancy words women like to hear than what I am," I say with a shrug, "I just need you to teach me what to say." Colburn is looking at me as if I have gone mad and then all of a sudden, he is throwing back his head and roaring with laughter. "This isn't funny," I mutter.

"Dude, this is hilarious." Colburn says with a wide grin, "Ulrich, the man, the legend. Isn't that what you used to call yourself?" I glare at his words as I remember joking with the others a time or two about being a legend.

"Fine, just forget about it," I mutter as I turn to start making my way back to the club, maybe this was a stupid idea.

"Wait, it's cool. Let's figure out what it is that you really need," Colburn says as he comes to stand next to me.

"I don't fucking know what it is that I need, all I know is that she says I'm a caveman. I want her to see that I can treat my mate the way she needs to be treated; I want to please her." Looking at him, I can feel myself frowning, "She thinks we aren't right for each other because we argue too much." Colburn places his hand on my shoulder as he squeezes gently.

"Dude, she's your mate and like it or not there will be arguments." He shakes his head as he looks at me, "you two are hard-headed, you will both have to find a way of giving in sometimes. You don't need to give your woman flowery words brother, all you need to do is tell her what you are feeling."

"I do, she says I'm a caveman," I mutter as I place my hands on my lower waist.

"No, not when you guys are arguing. I am talking about the way you feel in general about stuff. Speak to her brother, get to know her and try not to push her to do everything your way, do some stuff her way too."

I'm not sure she wants to get to know me, I think the attraction is there for her but in regard to personality I don't think my mate likes me much. I squeeze my eyes shut trying to block everything out; I knew having a mate was going to drive me crazy, I was right.

ANASTASIA 14

Ulrich can get under my skin like no one has ever done. From the moment I saw him that I knew there was something different about him but I would never have thought that it was the attraction that we have. It was difficult for me to believe in everything that was said to me about Ulrich being the one and only man for me, but even with all our fighting I know that there is something there between us that is rare.

Being with Ulrich I'm sure will bring a lot of arguments, him and I are just too hard-headed. I still think him a caveman as he just ploughs along taking everyone and everything in his wake, but I am finding that trait more and more appealing as he portrays the picture of male dominance in everything he does. I will never tell him or another soul that as I won't let him dominate me, or at least not all the time. The image of him throwing me over his knee and spanking me has warmth flooding my cheeks. That is a typical male dominance move from him, but instead of being repelled by it I was turned on.

I will never tell him that or anyone else for that matter but that man turns me on like no other man ever has, and everything that women have been telling me since they arrived I now am starting to believe. Last night I went to sleep by myself but during the night I felt Ulrich slide into bed with me. He placed his arms around my waist and pulled my back tight against his chest. I remember muttering in my sleep, but I didn't awake fully to enjoy it which now I wish I had.

When I woke up this morning he was gone, and I was once again alone in the room, but at least now I feel like I have a purpose and am not just sitting around hiding from whoever kidnapped me. I need to try and find which company is allowing for this trafficking ring to operate and steal so many women's lives. Sasha told me yesterday that Dora died, that her system was too debilitated by the time they found her for her to survive. All I could think when she told me was that that could have been me.

I will fight with these men, besides Ulrich's side, to try and stop these men that think it is okay to hurt women. Taking in a deep breath, I open the door to the room to make my way down to where I left the laptop yesterday. Walking in I see Dag standing against the outside door, leaning against the doorframe with a mug in his hand. What grabs my attention is his naked back, the muscles rippling as he lifts his arm, bringing the cup to his lips. The wings tattooed on his back moving with his action. His low-cut jeans covering a perfect ass.

"Morning Anastasia." His quiet rumble vibrates through the empty room; I tense, feeling my face heat with colour. I hope he didn't realize I was staring at him, but the damn man still has his back to me and hasn't even turned his head. How did he know it was me?

"Morning," I murmur, making my way towards the table with the laptop on it. He finally turns slightly and looks at me. "Where is everyone?" I ask, trying to keep my eyes away from his body, but it's not easy as the tattoos catch my eye. There is the face of a beautiful woman tattooed on the left side of his chest, her soft eyes seem sad.

"Most of the brothers went out, they will be back tomorrow. The others are around somewhere." He makes his way towards me, his eyes on the laptop. "Do you think you will be able to find the company that is trafficking the women?"

"I will try my best, depending on how well they know the system they might be able to hide their trail, but I doubt they could cover their tracks everywhere." He pulls out the chair on the opposite side of the table and sits down, finally looking up at me.

"How long have you been working in the shipping industry?" he asks with a raised brow.

"Going on to five years now, I was lucky to find a job with Mr. Smith." I shrug as I look at the screen, "even though he doesn't spend much time at the company, he taught me most of the things I needed to know about the industry, the rest I learned with time."

"I looked into your boss yesterday, do you know that he has a gambling problem?" My head snaps up from the screen to his face in surprise. "You didn't know?" he states when he sees my surprise, now some things make sense. The way he was always taking money out of the company for his personal use.

"No, I didn't," I mutter, thinking back to all the times he used to go out in the middle of the day.

"You practically ran the company for him, do you know that if it wasn't for you, he would have folded already." I nod, that is why he relied on me so much.

"I should phone him to let him know that I am okay and will come back to work soon, but Ulrich thinks best that I don't do it yet," I state and see Dag nod as he raises his brow.

"He is right, until we know how they found out about

you and if anyone helped them, it is better that others don't find out that you are here."

"Do you think that I'm still in danger?" Ulrich told me that I am, but I want to know what this dangerously handsome man before me thinks.

"You are Ulrich's mate; you will always be in danger." I tense, what does he mean with that? Will Ulrich somehow hurt me? He does have the temper to go with it.

"Why?"

"We have enemies' sweetheart and you have been identified as a target. They tried once, and they would do it again if they get a chance." I relax, realizing how stupid I was being thinking that somehow, I would be in danger from Ulrich.

"Do you know where Ulrich is?" I tried not to ask, but ever since our argument last night I haven't spoken to him.

"He went with the others; he will be back tomorrow." My stomach tenses at his statement, he didn't even say anything before he left. I know that I am being silly feeling upset about him not saying goodbye when he left, but I can't help it. Yesterday after our fight I was genuinely thinking of leaving, but each minute that passed and my anger subsided I realized that I just don't want to leave. I want that man, I want to be able to know that he is thinking about me and that he wants to be with me as much as I am finding myself thinking about him and wanting to see him. A thought pop's into my mind and I tense.

"Where is Tanya?" If they have taken the women with them then Ulrich better prepare himself because hell has no fury like me. Dag shrugs as he sits forwards to place his now empty mug on the table.

"You don't know, Monica and Tanya have been sent packing," he states as he stands, "we don't let anyone disrespect our women, they insulted you, they are out." I should be feeling bad about the fact that two women have been fired, if that is what I can call it, but I'm not. I didn't want the nagging reminder every time I looked at them that Ulrich was in bed with them before. I know it was before me and I know that it shouldn't bother me, but it does.

"Well, I'll leave you to your work, I will be in the workshop if you need me." With those words he leaves, I shake my head as I think of what he said. I hope I don't need him because I haven't got a clue where the workshop is.

I don't know how much time passes with me engrossed in finding something that would tell me who is doing this when I hear a noise. Looking up, I see Camille and Andy walking in, when they see me they stop. I can see by their expressions that I am the last person that they want to see right now but if I am going to be here for any amount of time, then I should make an effort to make friends. "Morning," I greet.

"Morning," they mutter as they make their way further into the room. I thought that they would at least sit down at one of the tables, but they simply walked through and out the front door. Well, so much for making friends.

"Hey girl, we've been looking for you." I jump in surprise a couple of minutes later as Gabriela calls out from the entrance. Looking over my shoulder, I see her, Katrina and Saskia standing there with smiles on their faces. I might not be able to make friends with the blossoms but it looks like I'm making fast friends with the other old ladies, it is just a shame that they will be leaving soon and then I won't have any other women here to speak to.

"When we went to the room, and you weren't there, we thought maybe you had run away during the night," Gabriela teases as she comes to sit next to me.

"No, I'm just an early riser and thought that the sooner I try to find something that will link the traffickers with any of the shipping, the quicker we might be able to stop whoever is kidnapping all these women," I answer.

"Well, you are going to have to take a break," Katrina says as she leans over my shoulder to look at the screen of the laptop.

"Oh, why?" I was hoping to get as much done as possible as there is a lot of data to go through.

"Because, late last night your man came to knock on our door nearly getting himself killed, I'll tell you," Gabriela says with a grin, "Bjarni doesn't like to be interrupted when he's being treated," at her naughty innuendo I grin.

"Eww," Saskia mutters, "No man Gabriela, too much info," she quips as she slaps Gabriela playfully on the arm.

"Why did he interrupt you?" I ask

"He gave Bjarni this," Gabriela holds up her hand where I see a bank card, "apparently he had to leave early this morning but he said that you are going to need some new stuff and if Bjarni would give you this." Why didn't he just wake me? Or leave it in the room with a note?

"I heard him tell Bjarni that you might argue, therefore, because we love shopping, we thought that we might help you spend some of your man's money." I shake my head in surprise. One thing is true I would have argued if he had given me the card. I have my own money and will not be taking his to buy myself clothes or whatever else I need.

"I don't need his money," I mutter as I look at the card that Gabriela has placed before me.

"No, no," Saskia says as she shakes her head at me, "Elemental's are driven to take care of their woman, you have to let him do these things for you." Then she lowers her voice, "he has been living for quite a long time, trust me when I say that all of them are very well off." I shake my head; I can't spend his money, it is just against the way I am. I have always been very independent, and I won't start now letting someone else pay for whatever I need.

"I will buy some stuff, but I will pay with my own money."

"Fine, but be aware that they are alpha males through and through, if you don't pay with his card, he will more than likely just place money in your account." Katrina says which has me frowning.

"He won't get my banking details to be able to do that." The women smile, Gabriela shakes her head in amusement.

"Sweetheart, trust me when I tell you that if Ulrich wants to know your banking details, then Celmund will get it for him within five minutes." I have heard this Celmund's name before, and it all leads me to believe that he is a hacker. Shaking my head in defeat I look around at all of them seeing their excited expressions, I have never been one that likes to shop but I do need new things as I am still using Tanya's clothes. They are definitely the last persons clothes I want to be wearing.

That thought has me nodding, which in turn has the women take over.

I am out of the club and in a car with Burkhart driving and Dag and Haldor riding behind us before I even know what is happening. Well, seeing as I can't go home yet, and Ulrich is only coming back tomorrow, I might as well enjoy my day with these amazing women. The longer I am with them, the more I crave the relationships I see they have. I know that they will be leaving tomorrow, and I will be once again alone in a place surrounded by men as Katrina told me that Camille and Andy are also leaving. Apparently, Tor has arranged with another Elemental's club to take them in. I have decided that I will enjoy this time that I have left with these women as I don't know when I will see them again as they all have children and don't usually ride out with their men.

They have invited Ulrich and I over for Christmas, but I don't know if we will be going or if I will still be here. I hope that I will, if they can be believed this thing with Ulrich and I is forever, I just wonder if it will be my kind of forever.

ULRICH 15

I insisted with Tor on coming on this run. He knew that I was just trying to run from the problem at hand, but I don't give a damn. I need time before facing Anastasia again, but being away from her the whole day has me going mad. I keep on thinking about her; I have never been so obsessed about anyone as I am about her. Not knowing what she is doing has me raving mad.

I knew that as an elemental we can't be away from our mates for long, but this is ludicrous, I have only been away for a day. Pulling out my phone from the back pocket of my jeans, I look at it for what feels like the hundredth time. "Just call already," Dane mutters from where he's sitting on his bike smoking.

"Phone who?" I mutter.

"You know who, you keep on checking your phone, just call her," he says with a shrug.

"She doesn't have a phone," I mutter, which I will change as soon as possible because not being able to know what she is doing is driving me nuts.

"So, what's stopping you from phoning Dag?" I tense at his question, then I shrug.

"He's not answering me." At my statement I see him frown and then he raises a brow.

"You mean that he's not answering you?" at his question I nod.

"How many times have you phoned him?" At my scowl he throws back his head and starts to chuckle, "You want me to phone him for you?" I start by shaking my head but then stop.

"Would you?" He shakes his head in amusement as he pulls his phone out of his Kutte and dials.

"Hey Bro," he says which has me approaching him, "what you up to?"

"We have just got back, damn women decided to go shopping," I hear him mutter, "so what's up?" he asks

"Just wanted to appease Ulrich, he's been

unconsolable." At his words I lift my hand showing him the finger which has him grinning.

"He has phoned me five times today," Dag mutters, "tell him she's fine, if she isn't, I will phone him."

"Will do bro." he disconnects the call, then raises a brow at me, "happy" he knows that I could hear the conversation from where I was standing, with our keen hearing we hear better than most. I'm not happy, I would only be happy if I could actually see my woman, touch her, but at least knowing that she is fine will do for now.

"Thanks," I grunt as I sit on my bike waiting for the others, we dropped the guns off an hour ago and now we are waiting to make sure that they get across the border without any problems. The Elemental's MC has an agreement with the Bratva Fury Mafia to transport weapons for them, that is one of our most profitable ways of income. We also rent out our services when it comes to protection for a limited time, Tor organized it with a company that has rock bands or movie stars staying in Cape Town for a short period of time and require extra protection for them.

To be honest, that is the easiest money we have ever done, yes sometimes the people we are protecting can be real pricks but its short-term gigs therefore we grin and bear it. We have one of those coming up where there is a new rising actress that is filming in Town and she will need extra protection while she is here as she hasn't got protection of her own.

I was looking forward to being one of the men on that job, but now I will gladly have one of the others take my place as I won't stay away from Anastasia for an undetermined timeframe. I hear the growl of bikes in the distance, which tells me that the others are approaching. "I'm looking forward to crashing for a couple of hours, I didn't sleep much last night," Dane mutters as the others draw closer

I would gladly ride for home right now, but I know that we won't be doing that and instead will be stopping over at another motorcycle club which we are friends with. They usually take us in when we are in the area, like we do with them when they are in Cape Town. When the others are close, I lean forward and start my bike, when I get back home tomorrow I have decided that I am going to try and be more understanding of Anastasia, I'm not the soft-spoken kind of guy but I will try being more aware of her wishes.

Dane and I ride behind Tor, Eirik, Asger and Garth into Town, the minute we stop our bikes outside the Panheads MC club I have my phone out of my pocket and am looking to see if a text has come through. I can't believe what a wuss I have become, but I have a drive within me to be close to Anastasia.

"Are you coming in?" Eirik asks as he walks past, looking

towards the club I grunt when I see Jackson and his boys. This is the last thing I feel like doing, hanging out with a bunch of bikers drinking and partying.

"Hello darling," I grunt before turning my head to see one of the Panheads women approaching. Great, now I also need to ward off unwanted company. I know that I have been with her before, but for the life of me I can't remember what her name is. "I was super excited to know you guys were in town."

"Yeah, exciting," I mutter, feeling anything but. "Why don't you go on inside sweetheart, I need to make a call." I see her smile as she places her hand on my arm, stroking her fingers down my arm, her bleached blond hair hanging loosely around her shoulders. The feeling of her touch has my skin feeling as if pins are stabbing into my skin.

Great, not only am I mentally repulsed by this woman, but my very own body betrays me. Before I would be on this woman like a rash, now my body gives me a rash if she so much as touches me. "Don't be long," she murmurs as she walks past. I look after her seeing her sexy little body encased in a tight-fitting red dress, but all I can think about is Anastasia in my t-shirt. Her wild curls springing around her as she glares at me.

Looking down at my phone again I grunt as I start scrolling through my contacts, stopping on one I sigh, well here goes nothing. I dial and wait.

"Hey," Burkhart greets.

"Hey, are you at the club?" I ask.

"Yeah, and yes I'll give her the phone," I can hear amusement in his voice.

"How did. . ."

"How did I know?" he asks, "well brother, I have a mate and I know how it feels when we are away from each other." I grunt, hearing that come from Burkhart I feel better as Burkhart is as bad ass as they come. "I have also heard the others talking about how often you have phoned," he says, and I can just imagine his grin.

"Yeah, yeah," I mutter and hear Burkhart chuckling.

"Hello," at the sound of her voice my whole-body tenses in pleasure, a tingling runs down my spine and I can just picture her frowning in confusion at being given the phone.

"Hey Vixen." When she hears my voice, I can hear her quiet intake of air telling me that she has the same reaction as I did at hearing her voice.

"I'm sorry about your room."

"It was in need of remodelling, anyway; besides you don't need to be sorry I'm the one that broke down the door and burnt the floor." At my words I hear her laugh, a husky sound that feels like it's stroking over my skin.

"I shouldn't have tried to freeze your tongue." I can hear her whispered words telling me that she doesn't want the others to know what she is saying, maybe I should tell her that no matter how softly she whispers, if there are Elemental's nearby they are going to hear what she is saying but then she will close down and not talk like she is. I will tell her when I get back home.

"It was refreshing," I quip thinking of the cold feeling I felt in my mouth when she tried to freeze my tongue, the grin spreading across my face as I shake my head at the audacity of my mate.

"Where are you?" she asks, "I can hear men talking in the background." I know that, that isn't the only thing she can hear. She is hearing the loud sound of music and most probable women's voices too.

"We are staying over at the Panheads MC club, they are having a party." Her slight intake of breath tells me that she doesn't like the sound of that. "To be honest, I would rather be there, the last thing I feel like doing is partying."

"Is it far from here?" she asks.

"A bit, but I should be home tomorrow afternoon sometime." I would rather my arms were around her this night like they were last night, and even though she was upset with me, her body melded to mine like a second skin.

"Ulrich." Looking up I see Garth a couple of steps away he inclines his head towards the club which has me looking towards the door and then tense. Shit, there is going to be a fucking fight and the poor fucker will die if he goes in there right now.

"I have to go, will see you tomorrow," I mutter, my anger rising at having to cut my call short. "Does he have a fucking death wish?" I mutter to Garth as I start making my way towards Tim, one of the Panheads members and a royal asshole.

If Tor sees him, he will vaporize the idiot. The last time we were here this bastard decided to pull a gun out and start shooting, his way of partying. A stray bullet lodged in Haldor's shoulder, which had Tor losing his shit at someone shooting at one of his men. If it wasn't for Dane and I hiding the fool, he would have died that day. "What the fuck do you think you are doing here?" I ask as I come to stand before him. His surprised look showing his complete ignorance of the gravity of his situation.

"This is my club, why shouldn't I be here?" he says as he takes a step towards me. Wrong move asshole. I stretch out my arm, taking hold of his t-shirts collar I pull him towards me.

"Because the last time we saw you, you nearly killed one of our men." He tries to shrug me off, but there is no way that I am letting go of this asshole until he is out of Tor's reach.

"Get your hands off me," he says loudly and then he makes a noticeably big mistake. He pulls back his arm and tries to punch me. I swerve in time to miss his punch, but my arm is already returning the punch, and he is flying back as I get him right under his jaw.

"What the hell man," one of the men from the Panheads mutters as he rushes towards Tim that is laying still on the ground. "You knocked him out," he states as he looks at me from where he is leaning over Tim.

"He shouldn't be here, take him home." Garth states as he goes to stand over both men. I have had enough of this. Turning I walk inside leaving Garth to sort out Tim and his friend. I walk towards the bar and take a seat, waiting for the girl behind the bar to come and serve me.

"What's up, I could feel your energy vibrating from all the way over there?" Dane says as he comes to stand next to me, a beer in his hand as he inclines his head to where he was standing before.

"I was talking to my woman, and I had to stop to go deal with an asshole," I mutter, which has Dane grin in amusement as he shakes his head.

"Don't worry brother you will see your mate tomorrow," he says, "Now come on have a drink," he grabs the beer from the woman behind the bar and places it before me as he winks at her surprise. I see her smile, which tells me that Dane will have company tonight.

"Hey Sugar, all done with your call?" I grunt when I feel her hands on my back, snapping around with such speed that she jumps, startled.

"Not in the mood, darling, maybe next time." I see her surprised look, but she nods and leaves.

"Well I never thought I would see the day," Dane says, punching me on the arm. "Ulrich turning down a woman."

"There is only one woman I want," I mutter as I stand, I might as well go to bed now because the sooner we sleep the sooner we. . . I stop in my tracks as I see two cops walking in.

"That's him," I tense when I see Tim pointing at me. No fucking way, I will kill the fucker. I see the cops heading my way and then suddenly Tor, Dane and Garth are standing beside me. The music comes to a stop as the cops come to stand before me.

"Did you attack this man?" the policeman asks, I can sense Tor's rage, his muscles are vibrating with his anger and I am hoping that he doesn't lose his cool because then it won't only be me in jail and I need someone to get me out.

"He was going to punch me first, I just defended myself," I state as I look over at Tim, my eyes I'm sure are promising all the hell that I want to reign down on him right now.

"He's lying, look at him" the other guy that went to help Tim says from besides Tim.

"Come on boys, this is just a misunderstanding," Colton, the Panheads president says as he comes to join us.

"I'm afraid that we are going to have to take him in, the gentleman over there has laid a complaint against this man and I'm afraid we can't ignore that," the cop says.

"You laid a complaint against Ulrich?" Tor asks from next to me, the rage vibrating in his voice which has the two men that are still standing in the doorway retreat a couple of steps back.

"I'm not fucking going in," I mutter, ready to lay anyone out that tries.

"Don't make us arrest you, sir," the other cop that is standing slightly behind the one the first spoke says. I can see by the way his eyes are moving around the room that he is scared that someone is going to come at them and at the moment I am tempted.

I will not be arrested; I can't stay away from my mate for longer than a couple of days before we start to miss each other's presence physically. "Tim, drop the fucking charges," Garth says from next to me, but I see Tim raise his hand showing us the finger which has Tor growl low in his throat.

"Come on son, let's not make this any worse than it is," the first police officer says as he looks at me.

"I'm not your fucking son." My whole body is tensed, my rage ready to erupt at the first sign of them trying to touch me.

"Ulrich, go with them we will be right behind you. I'm sure you won't be there long," Asger says from where he is standing behind Tim and his friend in the doorway. I know that they are going to intimidate Tim to drop the charges, that is, if Tor doesn't kill him first. I am holding onto my rage by a thread, at any other time I would fight my way out of this mess but now I have Anastasia and I will not do anything that will hurt her in the long run, and me being away from her will hurt her.

I grunt as I take a step towards the cop, looking over at Tor, "I can't stay in there long." I can tell by his tense jaw that he is holding his temper, but by the vibration in the energy that temper is going to explode soon. His eyes don't deviate from the cops, but he nods, which has me walking past the cops towards the door. I swear if Tim doesn't get out of my fucking way, I will lay him flat and then they will have a real reason to keep me in.

He must have sensed his predicament because by the time I got to the door with the cops one on each side of me and the other men close behind them which clearly has them uneasy, he is gone from my path. I know that the others will get me out, but will they get me out in time?

ANASTASIA 16

They aren't telling me something, Ulrich told me that he would be back today, but it's nearly midnight and the men aren't back. I can't stop thinking about him, I never thought that I could miss someone the way I am missing him. Draco and his men left today with my fast-becoming friends, I thought that I would be okay as I am busy trying to find a link between the ships and the kidnapped women, but I'm not.

I can't concentrate. Every time I looked at the laptop all I saw was Ulrich's face, so I switched off the laptop and came up to try and sleep but that too is not cooperating with me. I punch my pillow again and turn on my back. It looks like it is going to be one long night.

ULRICH

I was excited for Ulrich to come home as I found something that might help us with who it is that is behind the shipping. I didn't want to tell anyone until I told Ulrich. I haven't known him long but I would have thought that he would have phoned when he knew that he wasn't going to make it home when he said he was. That is one of the reasons why I think there is something that the men aren't saying. When I ask if they know when the others are coming, they become evasive saying that something came up.

"Aargh," I grunt as I punch the pillow again before sitting up. I'm not going to get any sleep, that is obvious, I might as well go downstairs and make myself something to drink. At least now I know that I won't run into any of the Blossoms as Andy and Camille left today. In a sense I felt bad as this was their home, at least it had been for a while, but Dag says that they will be fine where they are going as it is another Chapter of the Elementals and they aren't actually throwing them out.

Making my way downstairs quietly I head towards the kitchen, I don't switch on the light as I head towards the fridge. "Can't sleep?" I jump in fright, snapping around I see Haldor leaning against one of the counters with a bowl in his hand.

"Oh, my word, you just took ten years out of my life," I mutter as I can still feel my heart racing in fright.

"That only works if you're fully human," he quips as he

lifts a spoon to his mouth, only now do I realize that he's eating ice-cream.

"I am fully human," I state with a frown.

"No, you were fully human," he states with a wink. In the darkness it is difficult to see his features clearly therefore I can't tell if he's teasing me or being serious. "Now you are part Elemental, which will take away the worry of dying young."

"How old are you?" I ask, I am still reluctant to believe that they have lived for centuries.

"Three hundred and seventy-seven years." I gasp. "Looking good for my age don't you think?" he teases.

"That's an understatement," I state, which has him grinning, "does that mean that I can live as long as that?"

"Sweetheart you are Ulrich's mate, that means that however many more years he lives you will be right there besides him living them with him." He raises his hand towards me. "So, why can't you sleep?" at his question I grunt in annoyance.

"Don't know," I mutter, I'm not going to tell him that I can't sleep because I'm missing Ulrich, that's just lame. Turning once again towards the fridge, I open the door and pull out the orange juice.

"I'll tell you what, if he's not here by tomorrow

afternoon I will take you to him." My eyes snap up to his as I tense. Can he somehow also read my mind? The Elemental's apparently can bend their specific elements, they are also superior in other faculties than humans. Maybe they can read my mind and all along I have been an open book to everyone.

"Can you read my mind?" At my question he grins.

"No sweetheart, would be interesting though to be able to do that." I frown at his reply,

"So, what element do you bend?" I ask as I take a sip of my juice.

"The best one, of course," he quips as he places his bowl on the counter next to him and crosses his muscular arms across his chest, "Earth." I don't want to burst his bubble, but I for one don't think earth is the best element.

"Why didn't you go with the others yesterday?" I ask, trying to figure out where they went.

"We take turns staying home, when they come back then it's our turn, but we are going to be away for a couple of days as we have a security gig to an actress."

"What? Are you guys like bodyguards or something?" That is something I didn't expect a motorcycle club to do, especially when it came to the rich and famous.

"Yip."

"Is that what the others are also doing, security?" I ask and see him raise a brow before he nods.

"You could say so."

"Why are they taking longer, what happened?" I see him tense at my question and know that he is going to try and get out of answering. "I know you guys are keeping something from me, just tell me."

Haldor grunts as he raises his hand to his jaw and rubs his stubble there. "They ran into an unforeseeable delay, but they are working on getting here as soon as possible." Again, that doesn't tell me what that delay was. "But as I said earlier, if they are not here by tomorrow afternoon then I will take you to Ulrich."

"Okay."

"Now, it looks like you're not tired do you want to go for a walk or do you want to watch a movie?" I frown, why would he be so nice and try to keep me entertained?

"That's nice of you, but you don't need to worry I will just sit here for a while and I'm sure I will be tired soon." Before I have finished speaking, he is already shaking his head.

"You're going to be missing Ulrich, I doubt you will be sleeping." I tense, it's one thing me thinking about Ulrich but for one of the others to know that I am pining for him is something altogether. I know that what I feel for Ulrich is too strong to be a normal infatuation, but I would rather the others don't know, because if they go and tell Ulrich the man will be impossible. "If it makes you feel any better, Ulrich will be missing you just as much." His statement has me confused.

"What do you mean?"

"Mates can't be apart from each other for very long, they start missing each other to the point of mental and physical pain." Well damn, they could have said something before.

"Aargh, let him just get home," I mutter angrily. How dare he stay away when he knows what can happen?!

"Don't blame him sweetheart, him not being here is out of his control at the moment." I raise a brow as I lift my hand and point a finger at him.

"You know why he isn't here, so tell me already." I can see that he is reluctant to tell me why the men haven't arrived back but that is just too bad because knowing that this can become a mental and physical strain, I will insist on knowing.

"Ulrich has been arrested." I gasp at his statement; I should have expected something like this knowing how unruly Ulrich is, but it is the last thing that I thought had happened.

"For how long, and why?"

"He shouldn't be there much longer, they are trying to get him out as we speak but it didn't help that the guy he punched nearly killed me awhile back, Tor is out for his blood, therefore trying to get the bastard to dismiss the charges when Tor is just waiting to pounce on him has been tricky."

"Oh, were you hurt?" I look over his body but, in this light, can't see anything that might depict an injury.

"He shot me in the shoulder," he raises one of his shoulders as he speaks, which leads me to believe that it must have been that one. I know that these men live by another code, but when I hear how easily this man talks about being shot and Ulrich being arrested, I wonder what I have got myself into.

I might be feisty and to a point don't take nonsense from anyone, but I have never been one to break the law or to retaliate physically when upset, but since meeting Ulrich it seems that unknowingly I have started to adapt to the Elemental's way of being, when I think of the way I tried to freeze Ulrich's mouth it shows me that I am capable of the same anger, the same retaliation that these men are.

When looking at Haldor I see a hard man, a handsome exterior but a world of hurt that he tries to hide behind a smooth smile. I am touched with him trying to keep me occupied, Ulrich told me that his brothers would always look out for me when he was gone, and I guess this is one way that Haldor is doing it.

"Let's watch a movie," I murmur which earns me a smile as he inclines his head towards the corridor.

"Follow me." I don't know how long we sit in the entertainment room which I hadn't seen before but it seems like these bikers like their movies and games, they have a theatre with a screen that covers the whole wall, reclining chairs to sit and watch movies. They even have a popcorn machine which I found funny when Haldor got all excited to make me popcorn, but in the end he's the one that ate a bowl full of popcorn with chocolate raisins in it.

Halfway through the second movie Dag joined us which was entertaining as he comments throughout the whole movie like a little boy. We are now on our third movie and both men are sleeping in their recliners while I sit here looking at the screen but not really paying attention to the movie. It is touching to have such strong naughty looking men worried about me and going out of their way to make sure that I am fine.

I have never had people looking after me like I have had since I came here. When I first met these men, they had me in awe how so many handsome strong men stood together as brothers, I know they can be deadly but what I don't think many can tell is how caring and soft-hearted they can also be.

Ulrich took a lot away from me the moment he touched me, but he has given me so much more. The women that have fast become friends, their friendly and trusting disposition bringing me into their fold, making me one of them. I have never felt part of a group and always been a loner, but with them I felt a part of something. These men making me laugh even though my mind is filled with thoughts of Ulrich and my heart is heavy, their bantering between the two heart-warming as I saw the true caring between the two men.

I know that I have to go back home, I can't just leave everything the way that I did. I have an apartment that I need to decide what I am going to do with it, I have my job which I have dedicated many hours of my life and which now after everything that has happened I see a side to it that I never saw before. I know that I can help by continuing with my work, but I know that I won't be able to do it in my current position. Mr. Smith will have to make it without me, but I would love to be able to carry on this drive to stop the trafficking of women, children through the different shipping venues and if I can do that with my experience then I will give it my all like I have always done at work.

I spoke to my parents earlier on, told them about the MC and how well everyone was treating me, I haven't told them about Ulrich yet as they will be worried that I am throwing myself at someone because of the trauma that I have just gone through but I will tell them soon. I did tell them that I met other women that had similar gifts to what I have which they were surprised to hear but overjoyed to know that I have found others which I can share that part of myself with.

I know that they have always worried about me, that they have always tried to protect me from that part of myself overcompensating in other things so that I felt normal. The problem is that I never did, until now, now I feel normal, I feel like the reason why I am the way I am will be revealed in the near future and it is for a higher purpose. After hearing from the other women on all their gifts and what they have been able to do with them because of the support they have of their men and the others around them has given me strength to look at myself and see how I can help others around me with what I can do.

I jump in surprise as Haldor sits up, his head turning towards the door, Dag's eyes are also open but he is still leaning back in his relaxed pose but I can see by his tensed muscles that he isn't relaxed. "What's wrong?" I ask, my arms wrapped around my waist as my stomach feels knotted.

"Looks like they are back," Haldor says after a minute as his eyes turn to me and he smiles. At first, I just look at him not sure what he means, but then I am jumping out of my chair and running out. This is an unknown future for me but it is a future that I am excited to embark on, a future that might bring me heartache but after what I have encountered in these last couple of days, it is a future that will bring people into my life that are genuine and caring. Most importantly it will bring a stubborn, unconventional, rough man into my life, but it is a man that makes me feel like no one else has ever made me feel. A man that has my heart singing with the thought of him alone, a man that makes me feel more alive than anything I have ever felt before, and he may be a caveman but he is my caveman.

ULRICH 17

The minute I ride through the gates of the club the knots in my stomach start to unravel. It has been hell these last three days without seeing Anastasia. I have a lot to apologise for but the first thing I want to do is take her in my arms and feel her essence surrounding me, comforting this void that has grown hour by hour that I have been away from her.

It is still really early so I will try not to wake her, but I am looking forward to sliding into bed with her and just holding her close. I park my bike and get off taking my helmet off I place it on my handlebars stretching my neck to loosen my tensed muscles. These last couple of days have been a constant fight, not just because of being away from my woman but also with myself. The constant fight with myself not to lose my shit and fight my way out of that shithole had me in a fucking bad mood.

I tense as I hear running steps, turning toward the entrance to the club I frown until I sense my woman approaching. Before she throws open the club doors, I am making my way there. The minute I see her in the doorway, everything seems to come back into perspective. Yip, I am totally fucked, but it is worth it knowing that I have this woman as mine.

She starts running towards me and then she jumps into my arms and I swear that these last three days just melt away when I feel my woman in my arms. "You asshole, don't ever do this again," I hear her mutter before she is kissing me, I wrap her legs around my waist as I take over the kiss tasting her sweetness. Some of the men whistling, others joke as they walk past us, but I don't pay them any attention as my every fibre is concentrated on the woman in my arms.

I don't know how long we stand like this outside just enjoying each other's taste, feel and essence before I raise my head. "The others are all gone," she murmurs as she lays her head against my chest, which has me wrapping my arms around her, holding her tight against me as I make my way inside and up to our room.

"I'm sorry," I murmur, "I didn't mean to be away for so

long."

"Yes, don't do it again," she mutters as she slaps my arm playfully her head still nestled against me.

"Why weren't you sleeping, it's still early," I ask as I walk into the room elbowing the door closed.

"I couldn't sleep, Haldor and Dag have been up the whole night watching movies with me." Hearing that my brothers have been taking care of my woman while I have been away pleases me knowing that she will be safe and protected if I am not around. Suddenly her head snaps back as she looks up at me and I can see excitement in her eyes.

"I found something," she murmurs.

"I see so," I state with a smile, as I let her slide down my body grunting as she rubs against my hardness that is weeping with readiness for her. I see her smile widen at my reaction as her fingers slide down my chest, stopping at the waistband of my jeans.

"You know what I think?" she says as she looks up at me

"What?" I grunt as she pops the first button of my jeans open.

"I think that you are way too overdressed." And with those words she pops another button, that is all the encouragement I need as my hands lower to her burgundy knee-high night shirt, pulling it over her head in one swipe. Her beautiful body shining in the first rays of sunrise that are filtering through the window. Her nipples perky as the cool air touches her body. Her hands are under my t-shirt as she runs her nails down my chest.

"I need a shower," I mutter, as I quickly divest myself of my clothes, "are you going into the shower with your panties?" I ask, looking at her tiny black g string. She shrugs as she turns her back to me and steps towards the bathroom, but she doesn't make it there when I see her perfect ass encased in what seems like spider webs running from the centre of her g string to the top piece. Fuck me, my woman is a tease, but I love it.

Grabbing her from behind, my arm snakes around her waist as my head lowers and I am kissing her neck. The purr that comes from her throat has my cock hard and throbbing against her ass cheeks. She thrusts her hips back against me, which has my hardness rubbing up against her ass. Placing my hands on the delicate threads of her panties I pull which has it ripping in my hands. "Aargh," she gasps but I don't give her a chance to complain as I pull her shoulders down with one hand and her hips back with the arm around her waist. Aligning my weeping cock, I slot it into her body, thrusting deep into her hot, moistness.

"Ohh," I hear her murmur as I grab her hips with both hands and thrust deep and hard into my mate, losing all sense of time and surroundings. Her gasps and moans driving me faster and deeper as I feel my release approaching, feel her body tensing, her moans louder, my groans deeper and then her body tenses and she is orgasming around me, her muscles tightening, convulsing around my sensitive maleness. Bringing her torso up against my chest I lower my head and bite her shoulder prolonging her orgasm as I explode deep in her body.

My essence filling her, marking her as mine. Her head falls back against my shoulder as I thrust one last time. My hands moving from her hips up to cover her beautiful breasts, the morning sun shining over us through the window as we both enjoy this perfect moment, enjoy each other and this connection that has built so quickly between us.

Moving back, I hear her sigh as our bodies separate, but I can hear the rhythm of our hearts beating in conjunction. I know that our connection will grow more and more through the years, that our essence is now interlinked and that we will be able to sense what each other is feeling with time. For now I will have to ask her because I want my woman to be happy, I want her to know that she can depend on me and that I will do what I can to please her. I also want her to know that there are things that she needs to abide by when it comes to being an Elemental and that I will not bend on.

"Are you okay?" I ask as I kiss her neck gently.

"Mmm, I think I could just fall asleep like this," she murmurs which reminds me that she hasn't slept. Looking towards the bathroom I sigh, oh well, I have waited this long I might as well wait a few more hours.

"Let's catch up on that sleep, we will shower later." Leaning down I place one arm behind her knees and the other behind her shoulders as I pick her up hearing her surprised gasp at the action.

"Mmmm, I could get used to this," she murmurs as she snuggles against me as I lay her on the bed and slid up next to her. I smile at her sleepy words as I hear her breathing deepen. This woman can drive me mad with anger, but she can also make me smile with the deepest pleasure. She is my strength, but she can also be my destruction. I didn't want a mate but now I can't think of my life without her, her very existence has my heart beating with pleasure.

Closing my eyes, I feel my body relaxing as the beat of her heart lulls me to sleep. I don't know how long we have been asleep before the roar of a motorcycle has my eyes snapping open. Looking over my shoulder, I see that the sun is high up in the sky which tells me that we have been sleeping for a couple of hours. Anastasia murmurs in her sleep and cuddles closer to me, which has me smiling, my body once again reacting to her closeness.

I have had many, many women throughout the very

long life that I have had, but never have I felt this complete contentment that I feel now with her. I have had kinky sex, have had different women all ages, sizes and races but never has any woman pleasured me the way that this one does. When making love to her my body reacts like a flower to the sun. All my senses explode at her nearness, at her touch. Anastasia is mine, and anyone that threatens that will not live long.

"Morning," she whispers, muffled against my chest.

"I think its afternoon," I say and feel her mouth kick up in a smile.

"Good thing we don't have to go to work," she says as she leans her head back to look up at me.

"Yeah, maybe we can laze around in bed the whole day," I say as I lean down to kiss her, my hand sliding down her back to her plump ass which has me squeezing in pleasure.

"Mmm, the whole day is it?" she quips with a naughty grin, "what about food?"

"I will have to keep you too busy to think about food," I tease as my lips crash down on hers, enjoying the kiss until she suddenly snaps her head back.

"Oh, I have to tell you what I found." At her excited statement I groan, which has her slapping my chest playfully. "I found a company that is linked to various containers that are always checked by the same inspector in Dubai."

"Great, do you know if there are any future containers booked for them?" I slide up on the bed, my back against the headboard as I see her sit up too, her hands pulling the sheet up with her to cover her beautiful body. I sense that she is still shy with her body around me, I will have to convince her that her body is the most beautiful thing that I have ever seen and covering it is a sacrilege.

"Are you listening to me?" she asks when she sees the grin on my face.

"Umm, yes of course." To be honest I didn't hear what she said last as my mind was on her body, I better concentrate, this is important.

"Anyway, the ones I found have mostly all gone but there are those three that I mentioned."

"Which three?"

"I knew you weren't listening," she mutters as she elbows me.

"Which three?" I ask again, my concentration fully on the conversation now.

"There is a container leaving in the next three days, one in two weeks' time and one in two months' time."

"Do you have all the information for the one that is leaving in the next three days? Does it say what it is supposed to be carrying?" I will need to tell the others. If this information turns out to be solid then we might be able to close down the shipping venue that they are using to traffic the women.

"That is what first caught my attention, all of them say bike parts." At her statement I frown, "and do you know why that is suspicious?" I shake my head at her question, "because it's supposed to be a medical company sending the containers."

"Interesting," I murmur, maybe this is what we have been looking for.

"But that isn't the interesting part about it," she says as she leans back and folds her arms across her lap, turning her head to look at me. "There are more containers like those going out, but they are going to Russia." At her statement, I tense.

"Damn, that means that they can be taking the women anywhere in Europe." When it was the containers in Dubai, we thought that maybe we would be able to find some of the women if it was just in Dubai but if we start thinking that they are taking the women in through Russia and then transporting them anywhere in Europe we will never be able to find them. "What is the name of the medical company?"

"KER Medical Supplies."

"You are kidding me?" She shakes her head with a grin.

"Nope, and I looked but KER doesn't seem to stand for anything except of course if you think of Keres which you had said some of them might still be behind the kidnappings and trafficking," she says as she taps my leg.

"Fuck, the others are going to love this," I mutter sarcastically, thinking of their reaction when we tell them that the fucking Keres have practically been hiding in plain sight.

"What does Ker Medical Supplies do?" I ask with a raised brow.

"Well, I only know what the website says, and that says that they supply all hormonal and pregnancy tablets and tests." She leans forward, turning so that she can be facing me, "but you are going to love what their slogan is." At her grin, I already know that it will be something that will just piss me off. "Enriching women's lives."

I lift both my hands and rub my face in frustration thinking how the bastards purposefully challenge us, they know that sooner or later we would find them and this is a slash at us as if to say, *'we have been telling you all along you just didn't see it.'*

"It might be a dead end, but I thought there was quite a lot of coincidence for there not to be anything behind it."

"It's them," I state as I slide out of bed, "let's shower, we need to update the others."

"How do you know?" she asks as she continues sitting on the bed looking at me, I see her eyes traveling over my naked body her cheeks flushing in pleasure. If it wasn't for the urgency of telling the others about what Anastasia has found out and organizing for us to stop that container in the next three days, I would be making sweet passionate love to her right now but that will have to wait until after we have updated the others and have an action plan in place.

"It is just like a fucking Keres to challenge us from the darkness with their innuendos." I shrug in frustration. We will most probably find there are more of those stupid hints, but it's difficult to follow a hint when we don't know what game they are playing. "We are going to have to find out who the owners of the company are, and you will find that it will be another web trying to get to the bottom of that."

"Maybe if I go into the office, I will be able to go through the paperwork and see if there are any signatures that we might follow up on."

"No," I state turning around I make my way into the bathroom.

"What do you mean no? You do know that I can go back

anytime I want to, don't you?" Looking over my shoulder, I see Anastasia standing in the doorway with the sheet wrapped around her and a frown on her face.

"Yes, you can go back anytime but you are not going to because it is dangerous."

"I can't live in fear my whole life," she mutters, "and it might help, besides I need to go in any way to let Mr. Smith know what happened." Her persistence is starting to heat up my blood, I want to be understanding but I am not going to let her go back into a situation that got her kidnapped in the first place.

"We will be fine without that information; we can get it some other way," I state as I step into the shower, "are you coming in?" I ask, I see her tensed body and features, but then she nods.

"We shall see," she murmurs softly, but I hear her, and the tone of her voice tells me that she is planning something. Well, she can plan as much as she wants but she won't be going back to her old life.

ANASTASIA 18

"I said, no," Ulrich says angrily as he paces, we have been updating the others on what I found and I decided to mention that I should go into work to be able to go through all the paperwork and find a signature of someone that might have signed the order slips. Ulrich is clearly against it but it's the other's opinion that I want and besides what could possibly happen at work?

It is sweet how protective he is, but I will still do what I think is right and if the others agree with me, I will be going in to work if he likes it or not. The only problem is that work is seven hours away on the road and if I do this, I will again be away for a few days. That is why I need to convince Ulrich to come with me but he is being pig-headed again.

"What do you think?" I ask, turning away from where Ulrich is pacing and looking at the men that are sitting around the table and finally at Tor that is sitting back in his chair with a scowl on his face after finding out that the Keres are unknowingly provoking them.

"I think that you did a great job, we would have taken much longer in finding something like this, but I agree with Ulrich it is unnecessary for you to go into work and risky. Draco and his men will look into things on that side of the world as they are much closer, and we will look into things on this side." These men are so stubborn, how can they not see that the information might be on paper. "What I do need you to do now is talk to Celmund so that he can look into things with this company that is portraying as a medical supplier. He will get the details of who the founders are and where we can find them."

"Do you need us to cancel the gig with the actress so that we can help with this?" Dane asks

"No, it's too late to cancel now they are waiting for you tonight. She will arrive at the airport at eight, so make sure that you are there." He then looks over at Ulrich, "Ulrich sit down you are giving me a headache," Tor states with a frown at Ulrich, I know from what I have heard that Elemental's don't get sick that means that getting a headache is just a figure of speech from him. "I want you and Asger to go and have a look around the harbour, especially where this new container is going to take off from."

"Maybe we can look into the inspectors that are supposed to check the containers and see if they are getting paid to look the other way. If they are getting paid maybe Celmund will be able to track where the money is coming from." Tor nods his lips kicking up at my comments

"Tal, see what you can find." Tal that is sitting back, his chair leaning on the wall as he balances on its back-leg's nods.

"I just want to know who this fucker is that has managed to keep one step ahead of us all the way, we have caught most of the Keres how is it possible that this one has escaped us?" Einar asks as he leans forward, his elbows on the table as he looks over at Tor. "If there was a Keres big wig out there one of the Keres that we have reverted would have known about him we would think, then why hasn't anyone come forward and given us any information on him?" I see that what he said has the other men thinking, I have heard about how difficult it has been to capture all the Keres and try and revert them.

One of the women also mentioned that when they have captured a Keres and they realize that he turned Keres after his mate died, then there is nothing that anyone can do for him. Apparently, Elemental's will turn Keres if their mate dies and if they don't take their lives first. I look over at Ulrich that is now sitting next to me again, his posture still tenses a scowl on his face as he listens to his brothers, his friends. I slide my hand over and cover his fisted one which has him looking at me. This man might be a hard-ass, but he has a good heart and I am lucky to have been bound to someone like him. I look back at the others as they comment and feel Ulrich opening his fist. He turns his hand around and entwines his fingers with mine.

"What if he isn't a Keres?" I ask as the others are all pondering over Einar's questions.

"Not possible, there are signs that it must be a Keres," Colborn says from where he's sitting, "he knows too much about how to hide from us not to be."

"He is also taking all the women that could possibly be our mates, only a Keres would do something like that. A human would take any woman," Garth says as he rubs at his jaw.

"Is there anyone that knows about you and the Keres that has the power to do what this person is doing?" I ask.

"You know; she has a point we could be looking at this all the wrong way," Ulrich says as he squeezes my hand, "We have been looking for a Keres this whole time, why not just look for anyone that might be able to do this instead of looking for one of us."

"Anastasia, how did you find the link of the containers to Russia?" Asger asks.

"It was the same company, but also the containers aren't being opened either when they get to Russia," I reply thinking back to all the containers I looked at that had been delivered to Europe.

"Is it possible that there are more alias companies doing this?" Garth asks.

"It is possible but for now I have only found this one, I will continue searching. Now that I know what they are doing right under our noses I will make sure that I will find as many as possible." Garth grins at me and then at Ulrich.

"She's determined," Garth states inclining his head towards me as he winks at Ulrich, "you are going to be a real pussycat by the time she is finished with you," he quips as his lips kick up and he grins.

"No, I like the beast in him," I murmur with a straight face, "he could never be a pussycat." The men grin at my comment and before I know what is happening Ulrich has his lips over mine and is kissing me passionately.

"Enough, you can go back to your room when we are done, you beast," Tor teases, when Ulrich sits back in his chair, I see the amusement in Tor's eyes and the grins on most of the men's faces.

"You see; you guys never believed me when I told you I was a real beast," Ulrich states with a straight face, but the amusement is there in his voice which has me shaking my head. Give the man a crumb and he will work it, so it looks like a cookie.

"Okay, enough chit chat get out of here," Tor states as he stands.

"Let's go, I'll contact Celmund and you can tell him what you know so that he can start looking into who's behind the medical company." We make our way out and towards our room, "I have something for you," Ulrich says as we enter. I wonder what it is now, he gave me a new phone earlier telling me that I was to keep it on me every time he was away. He lets go of my hand and walks towards his wardrobe; he leans forward pulling a small box out of the back. When he turns, he seems awkward as if he doesn't know how to go about it. He lifts the box up in his hand, "when we are born our parents choose two stones that call to them, those stones are then bent together with the four elements to transform them into that babies birth stone." He raises his other hand to touch the amber that he uses at all times around his neck.

"With mine it was slightly different as instead of stone my parents were driven to a handful of soil, which when placed against the elements transformed it into Amber." I love it on him, in certain light it shines like the sunset. "When an Elemental mate the other stone that was transformed at his birth is then placed around his mates' neck to protect her with his essence." At the realization of what he is saying dawns, I feel a knot growing in my throat. I know that for him this must be a big step; to me it sounds similar to an engagement or even a marriage. He approaches, opening the box for me to look inside which has me stunned at the beauty of the Amber inside.

"Ohh," I murmur as I see the amber is the same sunset colour as his but there seems to be an air bubble inside it which makes the centre a much lighter colour. Looking up to his face I see his unsure expression which is endearing how such a cocky man can be unsure about something like this. "It's absolutely beautiful," I murmur.

He lifts the amber out of the box, the dark gold chain hanging from its intricate design that wraps around the amber. He steps behind me and then he is placing the chain around my neck, "I give you a part of my essence to protect and enhance your energy. By wearing this amber, you will always have a piece of me with you. You are now part of my blood, my soul, my very essence. I ask that you wear this always to remind you of our bond and the love that I hold for you." His beautiful words touch a part of me that I have held hidden from everyone, the part that has looked for love, that has looked for someone that I know is there for me no matter what.

I have always craved the security of having someone that I know loves me no matter what, someone that will be there for me even if I'm in a bad mood. Turning, I throw my arms around his neck, the uncertainty that I have held about him vanishing as I feel the warmth of the stone against my skin. "Thank you," hearing him say that he loves me has opened a world of dreams, of cravings that I have had my whole life but that I have held hidden even from myself.

"Now, let's phone Celmund because soon Asger will be knocking on the door." I had forgotten that he is going with Asger to have a look around the docks and see if they can find anything. "Hey brother," Ulrich says as Celmund answers the phone and then I see him grin as he looks at me and winks, "yip, I've joined the mated ranks." At his words I grin, to know that this man before me is mine has a special part of me rejoicing.

"Anastasia, my mate has found something in regard to the trafficking, we need you to look into some stuff and see what you can find." I don't know what Celmund replies, but next Ulrich is putting the phone on speaker and introducing the two of us. After explaining everything to Celmund and giving him all the details that I have found, he confirms that he will look into everything and get back to us as soon as possible.

When Ulrich disconnects the call I am excited knowing that everything that is happening is because I found this lead, maybe this will lead to them capturing whoever is behind all the kidnapping and the trafficking and close down the operation.

"Okay now I have to go. Be good and I will see you when I get back." He kisses me with such gentleness that I feel my heart tightening in pleasure. I haven't told him that I love him for the simple reason that I think it's way too soon, how can I possibly love a man that I have only known for such a short time? Is it even possible that these feelings that I am feeling is love?

I thought that I loved my first boyfriend when I was younger, but that clearly wasn't true because this feeling that I have for Ulrich is so much more consuming, so much more overpowering. I think of him constantly, his mere presence pleases me, his touch ignites feelings within me that I didn't even know I had. Is this love, or is this just passion? After seeing what I have and living with these men for the time that I have it is clear that what they have told me is true, but will I be able to integrate into their lives and be part of what they are, will be able to give myself completely to another without holding anything back because with Ulrich that is what he would expect.

Whichever it is I will have to organize my life that I left behind first before I can start a new one. Walking towards the bed, I sit down as I lift my new phone from the side table. Looking at the phone, I take a deep breath before dialling.

"Hello."

"Mr. Smith." When he hears my voice, there is a pause before he replies.

"Where the hell have you been? Your parents were here looking for you, the police were here looking for you and you just left everything and disappeared. I never thought you would do something like that." I can hear the anger in his voice.

"I was kidnapped." That has him pausing.

"Oh dear," he murmurs, "are you okay?"

"Yes, I'm fine now,"

"When are you coming back?" Just like him to only think of himself, I shake my head in amusement.

"I'm sorry, that is why I am phoning but I won't be able to go back to work anymore." I hear his sharp intake of breath at my statement.

"What! Why not?"

"I'm thinking of staying in Cape Town, I can't work for you if I live here," I state.

"How can you live in Cape Town; your whole life is here." I can hear the anger rising in his voice, great that is all I need to deal with a tantrum right now. "You can't do that to me, you can't just leave."

"I'm sorry with everything that happened to me I can't see myself returning to Port Elizabeth." I know that it will be a struggle for him the way he runs his business and I truly wish he finds someone that will do for him what I did but now that I have found Ulrich I can't go back to a life that I just existed. I have felt more alive here in the time that I have been at the club then I have felt my whole life.

"We will get you a psychologist; we will get you whatever you need, but you can't just change your whole life because of one incident in your life."

"I'm sorry Mr. Smith, I really wish it were that simple but I'm afraid that I have made up my mind and I won't be going back. I want to thank you for the opportunity you afforded me, but it is now time for me to think about what is best for me."

"You want a raise, is that what this is about?"

"No, all I want is for you to know that I won't be coming back. Please get yourself another assistant and I wish you all the best." I disconnect the call before he can continue, I understand that from his side it is difficult, but I now have to think of myself where before I lived for my work. Next, I phone my parents, I might as well get everything sorted today.

"Hello," my father's voice places a smile on my face as I think of his kind face looking at me.

"Dad." I can hear his intake of breath when he hears my voice, my mother had difficulties falling pregnant so when I came along it was a miracle for both of them.

"Sweetheart, is everything okay?" I smile at his immediate concern.

"Yes, everything is absolutely fine." I murmur, "but I was phoning to tell you that I'm not coming back to Port Elizabeth, I'm going to stay here." There is a pause after my statement, which tells me that Dad is pondering all the angles of his reply.

"Are you sure that is what you want sweetheart?" My parents have always trusted my judgement and I know that they will be concerned but in the end they will trust me to do what is best for me.

"Yes, I have already spoken to work and told them that I won't be coming back." I lean back on the bed and close my eyes as I think of my Dad's caring smile. "I met someone, Dad, and we are going to be staying together."

"Isn't that a bit soon?" I can hear the surprise in his voice.

"He is the man that found me, Ulrich," I state, "he makes me happy Dad and he knows all about my ice and thinks that it's awesome."

"You are going to be so far away," he murmurs softly,

which tells me that he has accepted the fact that I will be staying here.

"You can come and visit anytime, you two are retired there is no reason why you shouldn't come here for a while and I can come and visit you whenever I can." I feel a knot in my throat, it is true that I have always been close to my parents and have seen them at least three times a week, since what happened not seeing them has made me miss them terribly but I believe that once everything has settled, I will be able to see them often.

"Firstly, you guys need to buy a phone which I can video call because we are in the twentieth century and that phone you have is ready to retire." At my dig I can hear him chuckle.

"Your mom is not going to like this, but she will understand," he says.

"Thank you, Dad, I will phone back later and then we can make plans for you two to come and visit." I would love for them to come here and meet Ulrich, I'm not sure how the men and Tor will feel about my parents visiting, but I'm sure that we can make a plan. After disconnecting the call, I head downstairs meeting Tor on the stairs I stop.

"Would my parents be able to visit sometime?" I can see that my question has surprised him because he tenses.

"Umm, I don't think they will be too thrilled about their daughter living in a motorcycle club with eleven men." There is a frown adorning his handsome features as he raises his muscular arm to pull back his hair from his face. "We have two flats at the back of the property that we built, they aren't yet finished but they can be in the next month, like when your parents. . ." before he can finish, I have thrown my arms around his waist and am hugging him which has him tensing and his words come to a stop.

"Thank you, thank you," I say happily, ignoring his tense body as I take a step back.

"Sure." I can tell by his grunted reply that he is uncomfortable with my demonstration.

"You know what Tor?" I say, "You are actually just a softie under all that bluster, aren't you?" He raises a brow but I don't wait for his reply as I turn and continue on my way down the stairs. I hear his grunt, which has me smiling. An evil action brought me to this club surrounded by these men, and has opened up the gates to my future, I am pleased that they chose me to be kidnapped.

ULRICH 19

"Did you find anything?" Tor asks as we walk in.

"A lot of suspicious movement but nothing concrete, anything on this side?" Asger asks as we sit at the same table as Tor and Eirik.

"Yeah, looks like the founder of KER might be more difficult to find than we thought but that has been the usual with this operation. Celmund says that KER is a government-run company." I tense at Eirik's revelation. What the fuck does that mean?

"The interesting thing though is that when Celmund dug into the company's finances there is a large amount of cash being injected into the company from a private source."

"You know what I think," Asger asks, "I think that we are going to have a hell of a time finding who the real mastermind behind this organization is, the only thing that we can do for now is carry on fighting each and every abduction and try and find the women. For now, we have a lead that they will be moving something or someone in one of the containers in the next few days, therefore we stop that one."

"I think we shouldn't," I say which earns me scowls from the other three men, "no, just listen. If we don't stop it, then we can follow the guys that drop the women off and have someone on the other side seeing who picks them up and where they are taken to."

"I don't like playing with their lives, you saw how debilitated they were when we found your mate and the other one," Eirik says, and I know that what he is saying is true, but I don't see which other way we will catch the fuckers.

"Actually, he has a point," Tor states as he sits forward placing his beer bottle on the table.

"What?" Eirik asks a surprised look on his face.

"I'm not saying we leave them in the container but I'm thinking that instead of going in with guns blazing we let them finalize the transaction. We follow the men that drop off the women and once the container is on the ship, we take the women out without anyone knowing. We get someone in Russia to do the same, see who goes to pick up the women and then follow their movements."

"That could work, but we don't have much time to plan," Eirik says as he stands, "I will call the others, it doesn't help that we are down three men with this security gig," he mutters as he walks away.

"Well, I'm going to go and find Anastasia. Call me when you need me." I get up but stop when Tor calls my name.

"She asked me if her parents could come and visit." If she wants her parents to come and visit that means that she wants to stay with me and that she realizes that this is the best place for her. I was worried that she would try and go back home with all the talk this morning, but if she has asked for her parents to come and visit, that means that she has accepted that her life is with me. I raise a brow in question, it is one thing me wanting her here, but it is another when we get civilians here and they might stumble on what we are.

"I told her that we have two flats at the back that we still need to finish, once they are complete then they are welcome here." I had forgotten about the flats; they were Garth's idea, but we all got tired of the building and left it when this trafficking ring blew up around us."

"I had forgotten about those." They look decent enough

from the outside but it's the inside that still needs work.

"Well if you want your woman's parents anywhere near here, I suggest that you finish one of them." Shit, I wasn't expecting to still have to do that. Nodding I turn to go and find Garth, if anything he will help with the building after all it was his idea.

"Hey Bro, I need help." Garth raises his head from where he's leaning over his bike.

"What?" well doesn't seem like he's in the best of moods, darn, because I really need him to agree to this.

"Anastasia wants her parents to come and visit." I state.

"So, what has that got to do with me?" he throws the rag that he was holding on the seat of his bike and sits back giving me his full attention.

"Tor has agreed." He raises a brow but doesn't comment, "but only if one of the flats are finished."

"Well looks like you have quite a task ahead of you," he mutters.

"That's where I need your help, you the only one that knows what to do there," I state and see him shrug.

"Have you heard of YouTube, it's great to find out how to do stuff."

"But building them was your idea, I thought you would

be excited to help finish one," I say as I cross my arms across my chest.

"I would have been maybe a year back, but none of you were interested in finishing them." He grabs his cloth as he looks back at his bike and shrugs. "There is way too much to do there for only the two of us, anyway."

"Fine, I will ask the others to help," I reply.

"Good luck," he mutters as his head disappears around the bike again.

"If they agree will you help?" the only answer I get is a grunt, damn, I had to get him on a day that he's in one of his moods.

Walking inside I see Anastasia walking towards me. Her presence has an immediate calming effect on me which I hadn't realized before.

"You're back, how was it?"

"Okay, nothing happened," I reply with a shrug and then turn as I see Einar walking past, "Einar," I call but he continues walking, what the hell is up with all these assholes today.

"What's wrong?" Anastasia asks as she steps forward and places her hand on my chest.

"I need them to agree to help finish the flat, only like that will your parents be able to come and visit." I see her eyes widen in surprise.

"Wow, how long have you been back? News really travels fast." I lift my hand and place it around the back of her neck, pulling her forward I kiss her. I had a calmer life before Anastasia, I didn't have flats to build or worry about being home every day, but I also didn't have meaning in my life. Anastasia Is a handful, but she is courageous and caring. If she wants her parents here, then I will make sure that her parents come to visit, I just hope they don't stay long.

I lift my head seeing the blush that has tinged her cheeks, "Long enough," I mutter as I turn to go find Einar.

"Ulrich," I stop looking back at her, "don't worry about the flat, if it's not ready they can always stay in Town, I phoned them today to say that I was staying here." I feel my stomach tighten at her words, turning back to her I wait for her to continue.

"I also told them that I am with you."

"I'm sure they are thrilled to know that you are with a biker," I mutter knowing what the consensus are among the population about bikers.

"Umm, well I didn't really tell them what you did but they will find out when they see you and they will see what a good man you are." At her words I grin, that is one thing they definitely won't think when they meet me.

"Really, they are going to think I'm a good man?" I ask with an amused grin, which has her slapping my chest playfully.

"Yes, they are because I'm going to tell them you are, and you are going to do everything in your power to show them the man that hides behind all the bluster." I grin in amusement at her words. We really do have rose coloured glasses when it comes to our mates.

"I will be on my best behaviour," I quip.

"I will make sure that you are," she says with a playful glare, "now don't worry about the flat, I will get the guys to help. I am quite persuasive when I want to be." I frown at her statement; I don't know how much I want my woman cosying up to my brothers trying to persuade them to help her.

"How are you going to persuade them?" The thoughts that explode in my mind have my body tensing in anger. Instead of appeasing me she winks which just has my imagination rioting. "No," I mutter.

"Don't be silly, I will be much better at getting them to help you than you are." She rises up on her tiptoes and kisses my lips, "I will just tell them that if they don't help ill freeze them while they sleep." I pull my head back and look down at her in surprise only to realize that she is teasing me, this is one side of Anastasia that I haven't met before, a side that interests me. I know that she likes to tease me, but I thought that would only be sexually, looks like my life has just become more interesting.

"Don't ever try to make me jealous, you know what happens with that." That was the first time she called me a caveman, but the thought of her finding any other man to her liking has me seeing red.

"Yes, I know, but you should also know that there is no reason to be jealous," she says with a gentle smile. She lifts her hand, her soft skin like silk against my unshaven jaw as she strokes my cheek. "When you found me I was slowly starting to give up on hope that I would ever find a way out of what life threw at me, but then you exploded into my life and you have shown me a different way of seeing things. A way of life that I never imagined myself living, I was dormant, aware of everything around me but not letting myself live it." Looking down at this woman before me I know that I love her completely, I might never be the man that she wants me to be, but I will always try to be the man she needs.

"You bring life back into my soul, I always felt that I was only existing, but you have erupted into my life showing me another way of living, a way that has washed away my fears and blossomed with new opportunities." I see her eyes mist up with tears, "what I'm trying to say is that for the first time in my life I know that I'm in love and even though I know that we are explosive together I know that I wouldn't want it any other way."

Hearing her say those words, words that I wasn't expecting to hear from her so soon as I realized earlier on that Anastasia hides her feelings has me pulling her firmly against me as I crash my lips down on hers. We still have uncertainties ahead of us when it comes to the trafficking of women, it will be a long track to try and find the source of the trafficking operation, but we will chip away at it one go at a time.

What is important now is that I have found my mate, I have found a woman that isn't scared to stand up to me, that fights my fire with her ice, that is prepared to change everything in her life for us and that stands by me with all my differences. Anastasia is a rare gem among the pebbles, and I have been issued with her protection, with the responsibility of loving her and making sure that our future is long and happy.

"I love you Vixen, and I am happy to be mated."

THE END.

A MESSAGE FROM ALEXI FERREIRA

Thank you so much for reading ULRICH and ANASTASIA'S book. This is the first book of the Elementals CT MC series. I hope you enjoyed your journey into the life of these bad boy alpha bikers and their women. **If you enjoyed this book, please consider leaving a review. Reviews help authors like me stay visible and help bring others to my series**. Next book in the series will be *DANE*, it will also allow you to carry on following the other couples and what they are up to, here's the first chapter…

DANE 1

"Where the hell is this fucking woman?" Dag asks as we walk towards out bikes, Tor organized this security job to protect a fucking actress, but the woman seems to be oblivious to the fact that she might be in danger. To be honest the last thing I feel like doing is babysitting.

"She's already a pain and we haven't even started." I mutter as I lean forward to start my bike, this is good money for not much work, all we must usually do is babysit whoever the next rich and famous is. To be honest there is hardly ever any violence, the only thing that happens is a fan might get too excited and try and hug the person we are protecting, but otherwise these are quite standard. This one has been different from the moment it was booked from what Tor had said the actress didn't want any security, but her agent insists on it.

It looks like we might get a petulant little irritating female that thinks she's too good for everyone else, and that she can order everyone around. Well she can try but she will fall short with any of us because one thing we don't do and that is take orders easily. As elemental's we are above the pettiness that humans usually have the habit of showing. Nothing irritates me more than a defiant human being, no matter if the truth comes up and slaps them in the face but they will purposefully be defiant for their own ego. Well if this actress decides to be defiant, she will realize that she is dealing with the wrong men.

I twist the throttle of my Harley as we make our way towards where her agent is staying, if he wants us to protect her, he will have to tell us where to find the damn woman. After the constant search for the trafficking ring that is kidnapping women, women that could be possible mates to the elemental's I was looking forward to having a break from all of it and just have an easy job to chill out and not have to think about all the women that those fuckers have already been able to traffic.

We pull over at the Global hotel, apparently the agent prefers to be served but the actress wanted her own place to stay at while she was here in Cape Town. Luckily, the scenes she has to film seem to only need two weeks as that was the time frame the agent gave us. I am extremely unprepared for this though as I haven't even seen this actress's photo, but the others have been briefed. I was lucky to have been assigned this job as Ulrich was supposed to be here but now that he's bonded staying away from his mate for long periods of time is out of the question.

"What's this fuckers name?" I ask as we make our way inside and towards reception.

"Mr. Taylor" Dag says as we walk up to reception. It is clear by the receptionist that we are not the type of clientele that they cater too at this hotel.

"Good Day, how may we help you?" the way the fucker is looking at us makes me want to punch his scraggly face. Placing my fists on top of the counter I stare at him; I can see him swallow as he sees that we are not the wannabe's but the real thing.

"Call Mr. Taylor down here, tell him that the Elemental's are here." I see him tense at Dag's tone, but he reluctantly nods as he scrolls through his computer before dialling.

"Good Day Mr. Taylor, we have two men in reception asking to see you. They say that they are the Elemental's" he suddenly turns, his voice lowered so we can't hear, but being elemental's our hearing is way to sharp, therefore he could be hiding in a cupboard whispering and we would still hear him. "Are you sure sir?" he says as he glances over his shoulder at us, "they don't exactly look like the type of people you would want to see." Shaking my head, I stretch my arm, my hand closing over the collar of the fucker that thinks he's better than us.

"Ohhh" he hisses in surprise as I snap at his collar, the asshole is so fragile that he loses his balance and falls back against the counter.

"Now, what is the room number?" I ask, he better not give me anymore dirty looks, or the asshole is going down.

"two. . .two hun. . .hun. . .dred four." I flick my wrist which has him sliding down behind the counter.

"Thanks'" Dag says as we turn making our way towards the lift. "stuck up fucker" Dag mutters as we enter the lift.

"This chick is becoming more of a problem then we expected." I mutter, I just want to chill with no complications for the next two weeks and she better not mess up that plan because I need a holiday. Stepping out of the lift we make our way down the corridor until we find the agent's room, his door is ajar which has me shaking my head at the idiot. We are in Cape Town, a country rift with crime and the idiot leaves his room door wide open for anyone to come in and help themselves to his stuff and doesn't matter that this is a five star hotel, he will be robbed blind here.

Walking inside we stop when we find Mr. Taylor sitting on a recliner on his balcony, "come on in boys" I tense as I look over at Dag, do I look like a fucking boy? I am three hundred and twenty fucking years and this asshole is calling me boy, all because I'm a biker and he thinks himself above us.

"Take a chill pill" Dag mutters knowing that I would like nothing more than showing this asshole that he shouldn't be so trustworthy. Taking in a deep breath I grunt in reply as I come to a stop at the sliding door to the balcony. Dag is taking the other seat next to Mr. Taylor.

"We went to the location that was given to us, but your actress wasn't there." He nods, a frown on his round face.

"Oh, that useless PA of mine must have forgotten to inform you that Freya has moved." He picks up his phone from the table next to him and dials, "Julia did you forget to inform the Elemental's of Freya's move?"

"I'm sorry sir, but I have just got back and. . ." the woman is saying when she's interrupted by this asshole.

"You're a useless piece. . ." Dag pulls the phone out of the agents' hand, disconnecting the call. "What are you. . ."

"Look, we want to start with this assignment, and you are wasting our time." Dag states, "Now, give us her address and we will be on our way, and you can go back to berating your PA." I can see the man isn't used to being talked to like that, but he isn't stupid, he won't try his highhandedness with us.

He stretches out his hand for his phone, "I need my phone, the address is on there." Dag places the phone back in his hand, allowing for him to find the address.

"thirty-two Augustus Road," he states

"Why did you move her there?" I ask curious to know if there was a threat involved and why move her to that area? I know Augustus Road and I wouldn't exactly call that area upper class.

"Me move her? No it wasn't me, she's an ungrateful bitch, told me that she was moving because the house I got her was pretentious and that she didn't need a five bedroom house when it was only her in the house." He shakes his head, "can you believe that?"

Looks like this actress isn't as bad as I thought after all, maybe we can have a relaxed time while we guard her. I hear footsteps outside and know that we have company, "security is approaching" I grunt which has Dag nod as he stands.

"I would say that it has been a pleasure, but I would be lying." Dag says as he follows me towards the entrance to the room. I hear Mr. Taylor murmur in anger, but he doesn't stand up.

"There is two" I murmur, more to myself then to Dag as

he can sense them as well as I can. I'm an air bender therefore the variation in the air has me sensing its movement when someone disturbers it. Dag as an earth bender feels the vibrations on the ground which he would have sensed the approach of the two security guards too.

Stepping into the corridor I turn to face the two men approaching. "Stop right there" they say. I could easily disarm them in the blink of an eye, but I would create more trouble then necessary, I shouldn't have knocked the receptionist down, but it was too tempting to resist.

"Relax, the guy is fine we just had a meeting." Dag says as he inclines his head towards the room door.

"Mr. Taylor, Mr. Taylor are you okay?" one of them calls out, I hear the agent approaching the door.

"Gentlemen, what is going on?"

"Sir, these men accosted our receptionist, are you hurt?" the agent comes to stand before us as he shakes his head in his flowing robe, such a pompous slimy man. I hate working for people like him, if Tor didn't rip out our balls if we messed up this arrangement, I would tell this asshole to keep his money.

"Put those guns down, they were just here for a meeting. I will make sure to compensate your receptionist." The men look at each other then one of them nods but points at us.

"But Sir, you will understand if we ask you to please revert from inviting these gentlemen here again." Mr. Taylor raises his hand in peace.

"They were just leaving," he looks over his shoulder at us, "weren't you?" he says as he inclines his head towards the exit. Asshole thinks he is saving us, I feel like punching him through his pompous face. Walking past him I bump one of the security guards as I walk past, I see him tense, but he thinks twice before attacking me. I'm not a small man, if anything Tor and I are the tallest among the men, people are usually reluctant to approach us, as bikers, people automatically expect unruliness which in our case they will get.

Walking out of the hotel I see Eirik leaning against his bike in an outward relaxed stance. "You took your time." He mutters as we approach.

"Missed us?"

"The Desperados have been snooping around here" Eirik states as I sit on my bike, "looks like they after someone too." The fucking Cape Town gangs are always up to no good and no matter how much we try to stop them it just seems like they grow an extra leg and branch somewhere else.

"Well we know where the actress is, lets leave the desperados to someone else." I mutter, I'm on edge today, all I want to do is get to this actress, make sure she's protected and relax. I'm fucking tired of fighting, tired of the constant knowledge of evil that is out there, evil that is always searching for a victim and no matter how much we fight there is always more to find. I need to find my woman; I need to find the peace that she can bring me. I am tired, tired of the long years of loneliness because no matter how many women I sleep with, how many parties I attend there is no excitement.

When Ulrich found Anastasia I confess to myself that I was jealous, at first I felt sorry for him when I saw him fighting the bond between them, but then when I saw the connection grow between them I felt a gap in my life, a gap that only a mate can close. Shaking my head, I grunt, picking my helmet up from the handlebars I slip it on. Dag starts his bike and then sits back as he slips on his helmet, when mine is on I lean forward and start my bike, the familiar roar of the motor pleasing to my ear, the drum of the motor vibrating through my body.

Dag pulls off, Eirik and I follow, the ride to the actress's house is close therefore in no time we are pulling up outside a normal looking townhouse, everything about this place screams normal but there is nothing normal about this woman if the comments I heard from the others has anything to go by. Climbing off the bike I grunt as I look around, but the neighbourhood seems normal enough, what is she trying to do, hide among the middle class as one of them? I feel like a bolt of static rushes through my body as I approach the door, what the hell is wrong with me today?

I swear I need a holiday away from everyone, as soon as this assignment is over, I'm telling Tor that I'm taking time out. "There is someone at the back," Dag says as he turns to head around the house.

"Something is feeling off" I mutter as all my senses are in an uproar, I can't tell if its danger as I feel them all over the place. Maybe I should get myself checked because one minute I want to kill someone and the next I want to hug them. What the fuck?

"I don't sense anything?" Eirik says as he looks around and then glances at me, "except your energy. What the fuck is wrong?" He asks just as we come around the house and I freeze as I see a slip of a woman, her back to us as she bends down pulling out a weed from the ground. Her jeans moulding her perfect ass, that has my dick erect and wanting to burst through the zipper of my low-cut jeans. Her long auburn tresses obscuring my vision of her face but the tight cropped t-shirt she's wearing does nothing to hide her bountiful chest.

Something about her seems familiar, way too familiar. "Hello" Dag greets as he stops a couple of steps away from her, his voice has her jumping in surprise, gasping as she snaps around. Everything around me stills as I see her, her mismatched eyes, one brown and the other blue looking at us in fear. "Don't be scared sweetheart, we your security. Mr. Taylor sent us." I feel a pull towards her that I have never felt before, its like the tide pulling me in.

"Oh, yes he told me" her soft melodious voice feels like silk over my skin, every fibre in my body is now at attention. And then she takes a step towards us and trips over the small spade that is laying on the ground from her gardening, before she can fall I am rushing towards her, my hands are around her waist picking her up against me before she hurts herself. Her beautiful face turns towards me in surprise, and then her lips lift in a radiant smile.

"You're like me" she murmurs, her hand lifts and she touches my cheek with the gentlest touch that I have ever felt, suddenly everything that I have been fighting for centuries, the tiredness, the anger the very darkness that is my life lifts and in its place I am filled with a light of peace, a peace that can only be mine if given by my mate.

ABOUT THE AUTHOR

Alexi Ferreira, loves the idea of Alpha Men who take charge are possessive and care for their woman. She creates books that take you on an emotional journey whether tears, laughter or just steamy hotness. She loves to connect with readers and interacting with them through social media or even old fashioned email.

She currently lives in Lincoln, United Kingdom.

Other books in the Elemental's MC:

- Wulf (Book 1)
- Bjarni (Book 2)
- Brandr (Book 3)
- Ceric (Book 4)
- Bion (Book 5)
- Cassius (Book 6)
- Celmund (Book 7)
- Burkhart (Book 8)
- Caelius (Book 9)
- Draco Salvation (Book 10)
- Draco Wrath (Book 11)

Join her newsletter to stay up to date as well as take part in giveaways and just let her know how you feel about her books!

Link: https://www.alexiferreira.writer.com/subscribe

Printed in Great Britain
by Amazon